DYSFUNCTIONAL
COMMUNITY HOSPITAL
An Inside Story of Dysfunctional Employees at Work!

A Novella

MICHAEL A. APPLEGATE

Dysfunctional Community Hospital
An Inside Story of Dysfunctional Employees at Work!

A Novella

By Michael Abraham Applegate

Printed in the United States of America

Cover design and layout by: TheBookProducer.com

ISBN: 978-0-9721194-4-3

The characters and events in this book are fictitious. Any similarity to real persons, living or dead is coincidental.

TABLE OF CONTENTS

INTRODUCTION

HELLO MY NAME IS ABE ALEXANDER and my new book *Dysfunctional Community Hospital: An Inside Story of Dysfunctional Employees at Work*...is a story about an Urban Community Hospital in Chicago, Illinois. My new assignment was to write a short story about my healthcare career and hospital experiences: the dysfunctional leaders, employees, customer service, and unsatisfactory outcomes. I would like to reveal to my readers, the customers, hospitals, businesses, communities, service providers, students and you about the dysfunctional employees who were privileged to work for a medical hospital. I have worked in the healthcare industry for over twenty years, and with a number of exceptional hospitals and administrators, and it was an honor to serve the leaders, customers, and communities by utilizing my extraordinary abilities, passion, and purpose. In my endless quest for success, I've witnessed countless of dysfunctional employees, conditions, inconsistencies, and unsatisfied customers in the work place.

What is a dysfunctional hospital? It's a revenue-generating, service-driven business where the employees are presumed to be working and servicing the customers, patients, and community. It's an environment where the employees should be performing their jobs instead of exhibiting unprofessionalism, conflicts, misconduct, unfairness, disagreements, inappropriateness, harassment, infidelity, resentment, discrimination, opinionated beliefs, greed and the disregard for another person's success, which destroys a positive, professional, and productive relationship that should be functioning as normal as possible.

What is a dysfunctional employee? It's an employee that is unable to function positively, productively, and professionally in a normal working environment. It's an employee who continually showcases an abnormal and unhealthy attitude and behavior within a group of employees. Their abnormal behavior causes customer neglect, dissatisfaction, and ultimately a disservice to the business. When a dysfunctional employee is allowed to work in a dysfunctional environment long enough they start to believe that their abnormal and unhealthy interpersonal behavior is normal. They usually don't have any social, financial, or intellectual boundaries. If their abnormal behavior isn't taken seriously by the business leaders, professionals, therapists, social workers, educators, counselors, clergy and communities, it will damage a brand, their accomplishments, customer service and revenue.

Are you dysfunctional? Shakespeare said, "To thine own self be true!" I am a dysfunctional person myself and fought very hard about writing and naming a hospital, its leadership, and the employees dysfunctional and using the word "Dysfunctional" throughout the book. It's not my intention to be offensive, demeaning, disrespectful, abusive, or embarrass anyone, especially our brothers and sisters who are trying to survive and thrive in the mental health community. The word "Dysfunctional" is really utilized to engage, encourage, entertain, and hopefully get you motivated to take needed action and assist our hospitals and businesses by providing new solutions for the abnormal, unprincipled, and irresponsible employers and employees in the workplace.

My goal has always been to write a book about my dysfunctional co-workers and the damaging actions they've been allowed to unleash upon the other employees, customers, patients, and America's healthcare industry.

Healthcare in America is a multi-trillion-dollar service-oriented business, and it's time the service providers became the difference makers in it. In 2011, over 49 million Americans did not have access to any type of healthcare insurance or benefits. In 2010, the newly created Affordable Care Act (Obama Care) was put into law and has enrolled over 20 million new Americans. In 2016, over five million Americans still do not have any type of healthcare insurance and benefits. As the new American leaders, service providers, and change makers we must continue to fight for every person in the "land of the free," so that if they become sick, injured, or want to visit a doctor for a medical checkup, it can happen.

If an individual is fortunate to have healthcare insurance and benefits such as Medicare, Medicaid, private insurance or the new Obama Care (Affordable Care Insurance), they deserve the right by all service providers to receive extraordinary leadership, compassion, quality, and impeccable customer service by high performing employees.

I've worked for a diversified group of hospitals in my service-driven career, but once I started working for Dysfunctional Community Hospital, it felt like I was hired to not only be an employee, but also a news reporter, double agent, human security camera, advocate and undercover boss. My pet peeves are unsatisfactory customer service and disrespectful and unprofessional behavior. My hospital experience has shown me that the dysfunctional behavior that the employees exhibit in the workplace is allowed because of a lack of leadership, moral principles, problem solving, and greed.

The dysfunctional employees (who put the funk in dysfunctional) have provoked me to write this revealing new book, to inform America on what is really happening behind the doors of a community medical hospital. I pray that this book will become an educational tool for prevention, intervention and motivation for each employee and employer, to get serious about providing quality healthcare.

My new book will provide you with a new insight and revelation on the mind-set, culture, and actions of the dysfunctional employees who are paid to be the best that they could be and not the craziest that they could be.

I used to work at a psychiatric hospital in Chicago as a mental health therapist (imagine that) and would jokingly tell my co-workers that the employees are crazier than the patients because the patients knew their diagnosis, but the employees didn't know theirs. *What's your Diagnosis?*

Please let me remind you that my new book is fiction. The dysfunctional hospital, characters, names and events in this book are fictional. The ideas throughout the book were created from my imagination, innovation, stories, and experiences. So if you think you know the characters and stories you're reading about, it might be your dysfunctional imagination running wild.

Take a VIP tour with me so that I can show you a dysfunctional community hospital and their employees in action. Put your smart phone on vibration, grab a bag of popcorn and a bottle of water, and enjoy the most dysfunctional expedition of your life.

Welcome to Dysfunctional Community Hospital.

Most commonly known as Urban Community Hospital!

Enter at your own risk!

Chapter 1

THE HOSPITAL

WHO KNOWS MORE about working in a hospital than a marketer? I remember when I applied for a job at Urban Community Hospital. I was currently working for Lifetime Drugs and Alcohol Addiction Program and abruptly had to navigate my next career move because the business was closing. My mother told me that it's better to get a new job when you have a job.

I saw an advertisement in the Chicago Defender newspaper about a hospital looking for a marketing representative. I decided to take my resume to the hospital, so it wouldn't get lost in the mail. I informed the security guard at the desk that I needed to drop it off. The security guard was an angel in disguise and escorted me to the hospital's Vice President's office, unlocked his door, and allowed me to put my envelope with my resume on his chair.

The hospital administrators were supposedly wealthy, astute and only hired the best and brightest employees in Chicago and surrounding suburbs. It didn't matter what I heard, seen, or researched about the hospital. I needed a new job, money to pay my bills and a place where I could grow as a professional.

It took a week before I received a phone call from the VP's secretary to interview with Mr. Doolittle, the Administrative Vice President of the hospital. I was ecstatic! The morning of the interview it was raining golf balls, but I was still early and ready to cook breakfast, if they asked me to.

"Good morning, may I help you, sir?" The day shift security guard said while clearing a piece of chocolate donut out of his mouth.

"Good morning, my name is Abe Alexander and I have an appointment with Mr. Harry Doolittle."

"Please sign in and I'll call Mr. Doolittle's secretary for you."

He grabbed the telephone and started writing my name on a pass like he's done it a thousand times.

"Princess, Mr. Doolittle's administrative secretary said that you can come to his office. Put on this name tag and his office is to the left, straight in the back. My man, has anybody ever told you that you look like Michael Jordan?"

I smiled and said, "Sometimes. I've dreamed many nights of getting paid like Mike and dunking on NBA seven footers for a living! I played college ball, but today I couldn't dunk on a five-year old for a billion dollars. Thanks for the compliment!" I leisurely walked away singing the "Be like Mike" theme song.

Mr. Doolittle was one of the leaders, problem solvers, and cheer leaders for Urban Community Hospital. He was a rich looking gentleman, who worked for the hospital for 14 years. He was the CEO's father's right hand man. He stood around 6'0, had a big belly, was bald with hair on the sides, and wore a big thick "Mike Ditka" moustache. He talked faster than a telemarketer.

"Mr. Alexander, may I call you Abe?" I nodded.

"I don't know how I received your cover letter and resume, but I read it and was impressed with your experience in marketing, sales, and business development. I see you dress to impress. Is that a Wal-Mart suit? Just kidding! So you're a product of the community and a graduate of Northwestern University. I believe you can be a valuable asset to our hospital and marketing team. The marketing representative position pays $27,000 a year. When can you start?"

I thought, what would Richard Pryor say? "Mr. Doolittle, thank you for your offer to work for the hospital, but I'm already making $45,000 in my current marketing position, and I was looking for a raise. I really don't like to brag, but I believe that I can be the best marketer you have ever hired. For the last two hospitals and drug treatment center that I've worked for, I've brought in millions of dollars a year in revenue. I seriously can't accept an offer for anything less than what I'm currently making, but thank you for meeting with me."

We shook hands and he took a firm grip and stared at me with disappointment. I think he thought with all of his fast talking and compliments he could hire me for less. As I started walking out of his office, he stopped me and insisted that I sit back down. He called the CEO of the hospital and gave him a two-minute commercial about why they should hire me. He hung up and stated, "Abe I want to offer you $48,000 with a $2,000 signing bonus. When can you start?"

I was getting ready to get paid an extra $10,000 (was really making $40,000 at my old job) to work for the hospital in the community. Not bad for a natty headed boy from the Westside of Chicago. After accepting the position, I made a vow to make Mr. Doolittle look like a genius.

I grew up a few miles away from Urban Community Hospital in the Gladys Park area and never realized it was hiding in the middle of the hood. I was born in a dysfunctional family of six; my mother was a single parent on public aid and we were raised in a fatherless home. All of my mother's kids were born in a Chicago hospital, but not Urban Community. My mother taught her children that it's not where you were born, but what was born inside of you. She

We were born to raise a brand new bar! We were born to re-invent the future!

taught us that God lived inside of our hearts, so no matter whom we are, we were born to be an American superstar. We were born to raise a brand new bar! We were born to reinvent the future!

Urban Community was surrounded by closed businesses, dilapidated houses, vacant lots, expressive graffiti, piles of garbage, abandoned cars, broken glass, with beer and soda cans littering the streets. The owners must have never heard of an exterior makeover, because it was supposed to be an off white, but looked like an ugly yellow and the kids in the community bombed most of their windows out with rocks and bottles. It had a sign on top that read Urban Community Hospital, which was supposed to light up like the billboard signs on the Eisenhower expressway (the Ike), but nearly all of the light bulbs were out of order. An American flag was barely hanging on a pole next to the hospital, and disgraceful to look at. It looked like it had been through World War I, World War II, the Vietnam War, and the War in Iraq!

I remember when I was on the internet looking for new employment and trying to gather a little information about the hospital and I couldn't find out anything. The hospital didn't have a web-site and I couldn't find their name on the "Americas Best Hospitals List." Why wasn't Urban Community Hospital acknowledged with America's and Chicago's best hospitals?

When I talked to the community outsiders they thought the hospital was a senior citizen building, Chicago housing project or a drug treatment program. They called it a butcher shop. The doctors supposedly butchered the patients who came into the hospital for their medical needs. I really don't believe everything people say, but there's always a little truth in everything, so I wasn't going to deny my curiosity.

Urban Community Hospital was an accredited 125 bed acute-care hospital that had been providing comprehensive medical programs and services throughout the Chicagoland area for over

25 years. The hospital's sole owners name was Warren Pitts, Jr. He inherited the hospital from his deceased father, Dr. Warren Pitts, Sr., who was a very wealthy plastic surgeon, and spoiled his only child with a hospital as a gift for his 28th birthday. I didn't get a box of cookies from the dollar store for my birthday.

Urban Community Hospital was located right in the heart of the highest crime area in Chicago, and on the corner of a deserted block. A 12-foot chain-link fence with barb wire enclosed it. The fence was put up to protect the hospital and its entities from the community's urban terrorists, predators, robbers, thieves, and mischievous children.

On any given night, the hospital was in a war zone. It was surrounded by three of the fiercest street gangs. The notorious "Commandoes" were on the Westside, the coldblooded "Knights" turf was on the North side, and the heartless "Warriors" operated on the South side. The drug dealers, whose nick name was the "Dope boys," managed the leftover corners where they marketed and sold their deadly addictive products and perpetrated as the community "Pharmacists."

The weather could be sweltering hot, raining, freezing, or had twelve inches of snow on the ground, and the dope boys were out there, shouting, "Coke, Blows, Pills and Thrills, Park," advertising and selling crack and cocaine, heroin, marijuana, and prescription drugs to their strange and loyal customers. Urban Community Hospital employees and patients would look out the windows and see the parade of cars lining up for blocks to be served, as if they were driving thru a "Big Papa's" restaurant." Their addictive-hungry customers sat in their cars, blasting their music, and waiting boldly to buy their superficial "Happy meals." The community's drug trade was a million-dollar enterprise and open for business, 24/7/365 days a year. Just like a 7-Eleven convenient store, they never closed.

The police were called when the hospital's supervisor got bored of watching the community's very own reality TV show, or when the urban terrorists or dope boys started fighting, shooting or assassinating each other like in the movies and violent video games they emulated. The hospital's administrators allegedly bribed the police with free coffee, donuts and food, so they would stop in or drive around the hospital, to make sure the urban terrorists weren't harassing the customers, patients, and employees.

Urban Community Hospital looked small on the outside, but was large on the inside. It had five floors and the security guard's post was located on the first floor by the front entrance where the emergency room was located, which was frequently empty (other than the flies swarming around) because it wasn't a trauma hospital. The security guards were the first ones seen when someone walked through the big red steel doors. The first floor was where the lobby, reception area, administrative offices, senior citizens program, medical records department, and the business office were located. The business office was their navigational system, which was supposed to make everything run efficiently. The business office employees' responsibilities were to complete the patients' necessary paperwork, initiate lines of communications with the other departments, and to admit every patient that came into the hospital for service. Every patient admitted into the hospital had to have private insurance, Medicare, or Medicaid benefits.

If a person didn't have any type of healthcare benefits, the employees were instructed to send those non-insured individuals to the nearest public hospital in their zip code area. Urban Community Hospital was a for-profit-hospital and their mantra was no freebies (charity beds) allowed!

The hospital's cafeteria, housekeeping, and maintenance departments were located in the basement. It only had two elevators, and at times only one worked. The medical unit and surgery departments were located on the second and third floors of the hospital. The fourth floor had their Medical Detox Program on it and the fifth floor was where the Adult Psychiatric Unit was stationed. The fifth floor hallway had a huge wrap around window running along it, where everyone could view the beautiful breath-taking Chicago skyline. In the back of the hospital, the back door was often unlocked, so if the employees weren't hanging out and the security guards were not making their assigned rounds, it was an entrance way for any violent criminal to walk into the hospital, and create pandemonium, which by the mercy of God hasn't happened yet. Urban Community Hospital didn't provide any type of healthcare programs for children; their niche was admitting and treating adult patients, which became their multi-million-dollar gift from the healthcare heavens.

The hospitals "haters" were always in awe at how this community hospital, with hundreds of employees and located in the heart of one of the poorest communities, continued to remain open, year after year after year, even during depressing economical times.

Chapter 2

THE MARKETER

IN THE WINTER OF 1997, I worked at a psychiatric hospital in Chicago and a group of hospital executives was touring the adult unit, and I asked one of them what did they do, and he told me that they worked in the administration and marketing departments. I asked him how much money does a marketing executive make and he told me that it could be unlimited. I had a new dream to work in marketing. I switched my college major from Psychology and earned a BA degree in marketing with a minor in business.

Marketing gave me the opportunity to assist more people by promoting comprehensive programs and building rewarding relationships with community businesses and agencies, churches, and customers who needed quality services. I found my higher calling by working in marketing, which provided me with the chance to lend a hand to the sick, uneducated, and poor. Helping the customers or patients to become smarter, healthier and live a better life made me feel like a superhero.

My new responsibilities were to work in the community and discover new resources to increase customer admissions and revenue. The marketers whom I knew and used to work with sat in their offices, gossiping, reading the daily newspapers, checking their emails, and talking on the company's telephone, and making plans for the weekend. They always had a mouth full of excuses on why business was slow, but every two weeks they wanted their pay check. The bible says "to whom much is given, much is required." As a marketer you were required to work 40 to 60 hours a week and to make sure the hospital's marketing tools, market share, patient admissions, revenue, and customer service was ten steps ahead of the competition. My marketing mentor taught me a long time ago that when a business is not making money, the marketer is the first one fired and the last one hired.

My first marketing assignment for Urban Community Hospital was to market their four community health clinics located throughout Chicago. I worked for several stressful months and enlarged their awareness about the medical clinics, and eventually brought in new customers, which were the families and residents in the community. The new customers increased our Medicaid, Medicare, and private insurance business, which benefitted the hospital. The community residents weren't aware of the hospital's health clinics, specialty doctors, programs, services, and amenities like free transportation, lunch, and a small play area for their kids. Before I started marketing the health clinics, the hospital's administrators' business vision and strategy was to close them because they were putting the hospital in the red. After a year of focus, hard work, and guerrilla marketing, the medical clinics became financially stable and I became a superstar.

After eighteen months of making success happen, Mr. Doolittle offered me the opportunity to take over the hospital's internal marketing department. The two marketers responsible for marketing the hospital's programs and services were fired. Mr. Doolittle bragged about his new game changer and how I could sell flip flops to an Alaskan, a motorbike to the visually impaired and a fur coat to the devil in the winter time. He was motivating me and didn't have to.

Once I migrated into the hospital's marketing department, we upgraded the marketing tools, developed a new website and created an Occupational Health Program (OHP) to offer the community businesses employee physicals, treatment for on the job injuries, pregnancy tests, car accidents, flu shots, and drug testing. The OHP was first created inside the hospital, but was added to the four outpatient medical clinics. By working inside the hospital, it positioned me to have a better working relationship with the administrators, employees, and doctors and had access to a larger network to increase referral sources.

Field research was performed to find out why some refused to use our services.

When I worked in the field I performed the necessary research to find out why the community residents, (seniors, single women and married couples, and the men hanging on the corners, in barbershops or relaxing on living room furniture in vacant lots) potential customers, and referral sources refused to use Urban Community services. I asked questions and their communications were that they didn't like the way the hospital looked externally and internally. It wasn't contemporary enough for them.

I tried to convince Mr. Doolittle to paint the outside of the hospital, put out a few beautiful plants and customized awnings and signage, and upgrade the patient waiting area. Once the patients came into the hospital and was directed to the waiting area they sat on old white-rusted antique lawn furniture chairs, which reminded everyone of the plantation furniture on the TV series Roots. The walls were covered with dirty dark brown paneling and the television set only showed two channels. A patient jokingly said that the carpeting in the room smelled like soiled baby pampers.

Mr. Doolittle was looking much taken a back of my comments.

"Abe, we've been planning to remodel the outside, inside, and waiting area of the hospital for awhile. I'm waiting on the CEO to give me the go ahead and release the funds."

"Mr. Doolittle? How long has the hospital been waiting to get remodeled?" I wanted to say 400 years, but it wasn't time for a Black history moment.

"Abe, that furniture in the waiting area came from the CEO's fathers, fathers' house!"

"Mr. Doolittle, I can go to the store and buy some new, updated chairs, add a few modern pictures and give you the receipts to reimburse me. We can get the engineers to fix the TV or contact the cable company to obtain new channels. People love to watch their soaps while they're waiting to see their physician. I'll contact housekeeping to shampoo and sterilize that old green carpet until we can replace it. I believe once we modernize the way the hospital looks from the inside out it'll change the customer's perception about the hospital and make them feel more comfortable. One patient told me that she'll rather sit on bedbugs than sit on that furniture."

Mr. Doolittle hesitantly said, "I'll get one of the painters to paint the hospital, mainly the window seals after we fix the roof and put out a few plants. Go ahead and bring the waiting area up to date. Put the receipts on your expense report and I'll make sure you get reimbursed."

"I have one more request?"

"What Abe?"

"I'm going to update the pictures in the cafeteria, too."

"What's wrong with those pictures?"

"They have about twelve pictures on the cafeteria walls with George Washington on all of them! George Washington was the first President of the United States!"

Mr. Doolittle started robustly laughing.

"George Washington is the CEO's daddy's hero! Go ahead Abe, but if the CEO doesn't like your new look or your ideas, guess who I'm blaming?"

That evening I drove the hospital's van to "the store where hospitals shop" and bought brand new inexpensive chairs and beautiful abstract pictures with my personal credit card. I loaded everything in the van, drove back to the hospital, and remodeled the waiting area and cafeteria without any assistance. I put the plantation furniture outside in the back of the hospital, so the employees could have a place to sit and gossip, smoke their cigarettes, and review lottery tickets.

I put the George Washington pictures in the hospital's basement storage room, to donate to a presidential museum, or sell at the flea market or online. The up to date pictures and comfortable chairs made the waiting area and the cafeteria look like we were on the Gold Coast. The next day, Mr. Doolittle complimented me on the amazing makeover.

"Abe, the CEO and me went to the cafeteria for lunch and once he seen those beautiful pictures down there, he asked me who remodeled the cafeteria? I told him it was you and he said, I like that marketer, he's multi-talented. Good job, Abe. You made me look like a genius."

"Mr. Doolittle, you are a genius!"

Chapter 3

THE CEO

WHENEVER SOMEONE WALKED through the big red steel doors at Urban Community Hospital, they always wanted to know, "Who was the boss?" The boss was Mr. Warren Pitts, Jr., the CEO, the Chief Executive Officer, the Commander in Chief, and the President of an acute care for-profit hospital. The majority of hospitals in Chicago and suburbs were owned by healthcare systems, medical institutions, major corporations and physician groups. Only one man owned Urban Community Hospital and the final decisions were made by him.

The CEO's father, Dr. Warren Pitts, Sr., was a self-made millionaire who created his wealth by becoming one of the top plastic surgeons in Illinois. He invested a share of his millions by buying real estate and a hospital, which became one of the top revenue generating hospitals in Chicago. The Westside community transformed once the Caucasians started relocating to the beautiful, quiet, and affluent suburbs, which opened the floodgates for the minorities to migrate in. The community was always medically underserved and the hospital provided the solution to thousands of resident's healthcare problems. It raised the image of the community. Chicago only had a few for-profit hospitals, but countless non-for-profit hospitals competing against each other for the same customers. Over the years, a few of the for-profit hospitals went out of business for a lack of new customers, decreased revenue, and negative medical outcomes.

Urban Community Hospital was on a mission and it started with their mission statement: "To put the patients first and provide care, compassion and quality services. To change the healthcare population with preventative programs, wellness initiatives, and state-of-the-art technology. To implement community outreach strategies and provide exceptional customer service to the customers and communities we serve." Of course, the CEO had his own personalized mission statement and it stated, "To dominate the other competing hospitals in Chicago, hire patient generating doctors, build an unstoppable marketing team, increase the market share and patient admissions, and revenue, and make Urban Community Hospital the number one choice for patient's healthcare wants, needs and future."

The difference between the CEO and his father was that the father was a saint and married to the same woman for over forty years, until they expired. The CEO was an eligible bachelor with no children, a girlfriend for each day of the week, had a passion for his hospital making millions of dollars every year, keeping his gorgeous black hair perfect, and treating himself to a few cocktails after a hard day of work.

The CEO was 6'2, movie-star handsome, and had more business degrees than a thermometer. He resembled the former Governor of Illinois, Rod Blagojevich, but with a Machiavellian type personality. One of the hospital engineers told me that he had a tattoo on his bicep that read, "Bad Boy for Life!" He was a smart entrepreneur, visionary, perfectionist, and a trendily dressed businessman. He was a "*Mr. Know-it-all*" administrator with an ego bigger than the Chicago lake front. His car of choice was an eye-catching red Bentley, which he parked in front of the hospital. The CEO's leadership method was to hire former administrators and managers from the Chicago hospitals that failed and instructed them on what to do, how to do it and when to do it.

Every Monday morning his leadership team met to review the hospital's business strategies, their problems, the patient admissions, and the revenue goals from the previous week. He focused on how many patients were in the hospital and why the doctors were not admitting patients, and why the marketers' expense accounts were always so high and their patient admissions were so low. He could be very critical and took pride in reminding his management team of the significance of cutting costs, slashing expenses, firing lazy employees, admitting more Medicare patients and who was the boss.

The CEO could be very critical and took pride in reminding his management team of the significance of cutting costs...

The CEO arrived at the hospital most mornings at 7 am (Monday through Saturday) and didn't leave to go home until around 7 pm. When he went on a vacation, the only one who knew about it was his second in command, Mr. Doolittle. He felt that if the employees knew he was on vacation, they would slack off, take longer lunch breaks, disregard their job responsibilities, and eventually cause the hospital to lose patients. When the CEO attended medical conferences or events throughout the city, the competing hospital administrators wondered how he kept his hospital doors open, while their so-called "highly recognized" hospitals always experienced difficult financial challenges.

Most days the CEO was in his office, watching the stock market updates on his computers and employee's on the TV monitors. He would have his aunt-looking secretary, named Mrs. Bledsoe, page a manager to meet with him in his office to talk about the problems he wanted solved. He took pleasure in overruling a manager's ideas and decisions, mainly if he thought the hospital had to spend money. When not in his office, he walked around the hospital checking on every little thing, especially the employees who didn't want to keep their good paying jobs. He believed in giving an employee enough rope to commit career suicide, but if an employee got caught breaking the rules and hospital policies, he ordered Mr. Doolittle to fire them. At times, the CEO was approachable, but if he wasn't smiling or didn't speak to you first, it was better to keep on moving. When he communicated with the hospital doctors, he was full of zeal, but the conversations he had with an employee, vendor, or a patient was straight to the point. He never sweated the small stuff; he left that up to his managers.

One day Mr. Doolittle called me to meet with him in the CEO's office. My paranoia kicked in and my blood pressure sky rocketed! His office was small, dark, and mysterious. He had TVs and security monitors on shelves, and two huge paintings of George Washington and his father hanging on the wall above his desk.

The CEO started the conversation and said, "Abe, have a seat, would you like a soda or a bottle of water?"

I couldn't believe that I was sitting in the CEO's office. I couldn't wait to tell my mother.

"Afternoon gentlemen, a bottle of water would be nice."

"Abe, I have marketers and business consultants working for me that a lot of employees don't know about. I must say your marketing and work ethic is one of a kind."

The CEO was too cool for school and knew how to butter my bread.

Mr. Doolittle spoke up and said, "Abe, we have a new marketing position we want to offer you with some new responsibilities. We hope that you know we appreciate your commitment to the hospital, and how you have taken the marketing department to the next level."

"Thank you!"

"I must say in basketball terminology, that you've been averaging triple doubles with your patient admissions, referrals, and relationship building skills, so we want to promote you to be the hospital's new Director of Marketing, how about it?"

"May I ask how much money will I make?"

I was expressing myself as if I was the man.

"An extra $15,000 on your base salary a year, a better office, lap top, and that new smart phone everybody is buying. What do you say?"

"I accept!"

"But we need you to do us a favor."

I started mumbling to myself. A favor, I knew it, once they gave me a promotion it was going to be too good to be true. I'm going to have to get to work early, stay late and make the 40-hour work week seem like child's play. Whatever, it's money-making time and I'm the man for the job.

Mr. Doolittle didn't miss a beat and continued with the conversation, "We terminated the outside consulting group that we had managing our Drug Treatment program to cut our losses. We need you to market that program for us with your other duties, and increase the program's patient admissions. I remembered you had experience in marketing substance abuse treatment. We need you to help us attain some new results with the drug and alcohol program. Get familiar with the employees on the unit and the program and go to work."

"Is there a bonus in it for me? I haven't received a bonus since I started working here."

The CEO yelled, "Abe, we just gave you a promotion and a raise. What do those TV preachers like to say…Count your blessings?"

Mr. Doolittle, immediately jumped in the conversation and said, "Of course we're going to structure a new bonus plan for you, so don't worry about it. I'll put everything in writing."

A few weeks later, as I was transitioning into my new role as the Director of Marketing, and standing in the hallway talking to a co-worker, out the corner of my eye I had seen the CEO approaching us.

He was moving gracefully through the hospital like a lion seeking his prey.

"Good afternoon Mr. Pitts, how are you doing, today?"

"I'm not happy! We don't have any patients. We need more patients! Abe, how many patients do you have coming in today?"

Chapter 4

THE CUSTOMERS

MR. DOOLITTLE USED TO OFTEN SAY, "Marketers are only good as their last patient admission." As the new Director of Marketing, I worked in the marketing department on Mondays and Fridays, and Tuesdays, Wednesdays, and Thursdays in the community. The goals remained the same: to increase customer admissions, our image, and profits. My plan was to visit at least three to five contacts a day. The administrators wouldn't allow me to hire another marketer to assist me in the marketing department or in the field, so unlike Captain Kirk of the "Star Trek Enterprise" there was no Mr. Spock to help me accomplish my goals.

I developed new customers by building friendship-type relationships with them. I tried to meet with everyone: ministers of churches, presidents of businesses, human resource representatives, social workers, and community service providers. I visited homeless shelters, public health agencies, drug treatment programs, methadone clinics, and the CHA (Chicago Housing Authority) buildings where most seniors lived.

I traveled everywhere trying to find new customers and visited the competitions medical clinics to interact with their employees and doctors. My new plan was to recruit their doctors to join our hospital's medical team and to bring their patients with them. I had to leave my ego in the car and walk block-to-block and door-to-door, speaking to the community residents

> The secret to developing a rewarding relationship with the customer was giving them what they wanted.

and placing my marketing fliers in their hands. Sometimes I'd put my marketing fliers in a resident's mail box, which was a federal offense, but since there never was any police around, I took my chances. I created large florescent fliers and posters about our programs and services, with my phone number on them and put them up at night, in the bus stops shelters, on trees, and nailed them on wooden light poles. I would do anything to keep my bosses happy, attract new customers, obtain my marketing quota, and accumulate my bonuses. Once the customers started calling me and knew that I wasn't the typical solicitor, they would in time utilize our hospital for their healthcare needs.

The secret to developing a rewarding relationship with the customer was giving them what they wanted. They wanted respect, professionalism, effective communications, personal attention, fast service, kindness, a hello, and a friendly smile. They wanted confidentiality, answers, safety, team work, cleanliness, diversity, quality products and programs, a positive experience, amazing outcomes, a thank you, and really to be treated like they're human beings.

Urban Community and their employees weren't giving the customers what they wanted and deserved. The customers seriously believed that we didn't care about their wants, needs and desires, only if they could pay for their healthcare services. When you work with the customers you have to ask pertinent questions and listen to get the answers. Some of their comments and concerns were very disturbing. They communicated that: "The employees are lazy, they never smile, they never say hello, and they're always rude!"

"I wouldn't send my ex-husband to your hospital and I hate his guts!"

"I was referred there to get an x-ray on my foot and the doctor operated on the both of my feet and now I'm in a wheel chair. You think I'm lying? Look at my ugly feet. I can't wear flip flops anymore!"

"I don't like your hospital because it doesn't like kids. This community is filled with kids who get sick!"

"Eighteen people got shot last week-end and nine of them died. The first responders couldn't transport the victims to your hospital because you don't have a Trauma center!"

"Do they still have that plantation-looking furniture in their waiting area? Why do they have pictures of George Washington all over that hospital?"

"I thought they were closed and if not, they should be!"

"My daughter went down there to sell her Girl Scout cookies and they told her no soliciting and if she came back they'll call the police. They scarred my baby for life!"

"They say what would Jesus do? Jesus wouldn't recommend your hospital to the devil!"

It became heartbreaking to hear so many community residents and potential customers complaining about the hospital I represented. Their negative comments and the word of mouth throughout the community were destroying the hospital's image. They made me re-evaluate my goals and responsibilities as a marketer and product of the community. My new mission was to try and make the necessary changes and win back the customers in the community, whom deserved better. Every day I had to drive through the dangerous streets and communities of Chicago, dodging the gangs, dope dealers, and potholes, trying to help the customers and stay alive. It was the potholes which reminded me of the disparities in America's healthcare system. One night while browsing the internet for new ideas, I discovered a number of alarming healthcare disparities and statistics that was destroying not only America, but the citizens and customers. The facts say that:

- Nearly 45% of African-Americans do not have a regular doctor. In contrast, only 15% of White Americans do not have a regular doctor.

- Millions of Americans are uninsured and African-Americans and Hispanics are the most likely to be the ones who are uninsured.

- Obesity is a major risk factor for cardiovascular disease including hypertension and diabetes, strokes, and cancer of the breast, colon, and prostate.

- There are well demonstrative studies to reveal that African-Americans receive a lower quality of care in many areas in cardiovascular care, diabetes, surgery care, and early diagnostics of cancer.

- More than 2.5 million African-Americans have diabetes.

- More teenagers and young adults die from suicide than from cancer, heart disease, AIDS, birth detects, stroke, pneumonia, influenza, and chronic lung disease.

- African-Americans are 14% of the nation's population and account for 60% annually of new HIV infections. A quarter of these new infections are among people under 24 years of age.

- 76% of Americans cited that money and work are the leading cause of their stress.

- African-Americans are three times more likely to be hospitalized and also three times more likely to die from asthma.

- More than 16% of strokes are associated with obesity.

- 70% of African-American adults do not participate in light, moderate or vigorous physical activity regularly as opposed to 30% of White Americans.

Those were a few of the facts and statistics that renewed my insight into the disparities which were plaguing American citizens, our customers, communities, and healthcare system. Urban Community Hospital was experiencing a number of serious dysfunctional problems, but the majority of Americans and the customers wouldn't need medical care if they took better care of their health. Why were they living unhealthy lifestyles, lacking pertinent medical information, not educating themselves about the medical challenges they were facing, and didn't have the needed healthcare benefits to live healthier and more productive lives? Why were they abusing drugs, alcohol, and smoking cigarettes and cigars as coping skills? Why were they dying from ignorance, self-destruction, low self-worth and discrimination? After communicating with the customers in the community and learning about the healthcare disparities, I wrote a proposal and a detailed report to give to my supervisor.

"Mr. Doolittle, I was out in the community communicating with a number of potential customers, and they expressed their concerns about their negative experiences with the hospital. They were dissatisfied with the employees, their medical treatment, and especially our customer service. Here's a proposal and report for you to read and hopefully we can make a few necessary changes with their dissatisfaction with the hospital."

While reviewing the report, Mr. Doolittle said frowning, "Negative complaints will always affect our image in the community and decrease the bottom line. Some of our employees and managers will be fired once the CEO reads your findings. What are your recommendations?"

"To create and facilitate customer service training for the hospital employees, immediately."

"That's a terrific idea, Abe!" Mr. Doolittle said, looking thrilled.

"I'll read the other ideas in your proposal and give me a few dates and times so we can get started with the customer service training."

"Thank you!"

Chapter 5

THE BUSINESS OFFICE

ONE BEAUTIFUL SUN SHINING MORNING, I was at work walking through the hospital and peeked in the waiting area.

Talking to myself, "This is what I'm talking about. Patients are everywhere. We must be giving away something free? I thought they took 'free' out the dictionary!"

I spoke to the waiting patients, "Good morning family!"

"Good morning! Hello! Who's that?" The patients responded.

I strolled into the business office and said, "Good morning super team! Good morning Tonia."

Tonia, the director of the hospitals business office was sitting at her desk in the corner of a messy office and spoke to me with anticipation, "What's up Abe? How can I help the man with the plan?"

"Tonia, your team is looking busier than the panhandlers on Roosevelt Road. I need your assistance because two of my patients have just arrived with the transportation drivers. We need to get them registered so they can be admitted."

"Be patient, Abe! It'll take a while because two of my minimal wage employees called in sick today. They're not sick; they just don't come to work the Monday after payday. They party for two days and rest on the third day. The day they're supposed to be working."

Tonia stops and answers the telephone, "Crazy Community Hospital. I meant Urban Community Hospital. May I help you, please...Hold on!" After she transferred the call, we continued with our dialogue.

"Abe, do you have the patient's picture ID's, Medicare, Medicaid, insurance cards, or are they paying out of pocket? Please don't say free!"

"Tonia, they're here for the Drug Treatment program and here are their Medicaid cards. Can you hurry up and admit them; they're going through withdrawals."

Tonia laughs and starts pointing her finger, rolling her eyes and shaking her head and says, "So you want me to jump when you ask me to do something for you? Tell your buddies to stop going to "Heroin City." Tell them no pain, no gain. But of course you can't hurt their feelings because you wouldn't have any patients. I know how it goes in the marketing world-no patients, no job! Make me a copy of their Medicaid cards and ID and don't take forever to do it! How does that sound? It isn't funny listening to my sarcastic remarks, is it? My team has to listen to those types of demands, every day. That's another reason why my employees don't come to work." Still pointing and snapping her fingers and rolling her eyes.

I told the patients in an apologetic type of way to, "Please have a seat in the waiting area and they'll call you in about 30 minutes to admit you."

"Thanks, Mr. Alexander!"

Tonia Lovett was an eye-catching, voluptuous woman, who stood about 5'9, and her signature look was styling in a long platinum blond Tina Turner Weave. She had personality plus, and loved to entertain her co-workers and the vendors with her sexually explicit jokes. She was one of the hospital wire's juiciest gossipers. She hung out at a table in the back of the cafeteria, always laughing loud, signifying and talking about everybody, everything, and who's dating who. If the hospital was a reality talk show Tonia would definitely be the host.

When a marketer received referrals from their referral network and the patients arrived, they were escorted by the hospital volunteers to the business office to be admitted. The business office was the hospitals navigational system, where the admission department employees and the telephone switch boards were located. The hospitals switch board operator was whoever answered the telephone first. If a caller needed to know an employee's phone extension, a phone number for a patient's room, or have a doctor paged, the employees had to look on the side wall where all kinds of papers and memos were taped. Speed, organization and confidentiality were not their strengths.

The business office employees who worked on the second shift may have been the laziest, craziest and greediest employees in the hospital. After Tonia went home they didn't have any supervision, so they would do whatever they pleased, which at times was absolutely nothing. They let the switch board telephone ring five to ten times before answering it. At times they didn't answer the phone. The hospital didn't have voicemail. The CEO always tried to save a dollar and since the employees weren't picking up the telephone in a timely manner, why would they call a customer back. First impression is everything, but only to the ones who believed in it or wanted to be a top ten hospital.

First impression is everything, but only to the ones who believed in it or wanted to be a top ten hospital.

Most evenings you could find the hospital's housekeepers or security guards hanging out in the business office. A memo by the administration stated "No loitering, eating, or food at the desk" but they were always eating a buffet of buffalo chicken wings, tacos, Chinese food, or arena-sized pizzas. The radio would be blasting and if anyone dared to say anything to the employees regarding their actions, they would go ballistic, like they were on the *Jerry Springer* show. Because of their "don't care attitudes" the patients had to wait and better not whine.

The business office employees were also responsible for putting the patient's information in the hospital's computer data base. The department lacked teamwork, so the billing was always behind, payments weren't being coded, and the hospital was late on receiving payments. Let me be clear, the hospital was not the employee's, so they didn't care and still expected their paycheck every two weeks. Urban Community didn't have direct deposit for their employees.

The business office employees didn't wear matching uniforms, so they wore their street clothes to work in. They dressed as if they were auditioning for *The Community's Next Hot Models!*

One day I asked Tonia, "Why don't your team answer the telephone in a timely manner with a professional greeting?"

"Abe, we work in the hood, not the Holiday Inn. We keep it real in the hood."

As I was listening to her I realized where her employees got their unrealistic attitudes from.

I asked her, "Why do the patients have to wait for hours to be admitted and escorted to their rooms?"

"Stop worrying about the customers. They know us and still love how we treat them."

"What if the CEO had an undercover customer to come in and seen the way your employees conducted themselves?"

"The CEO doesn't care! He comes in here four or five times a day to look in that yellow admissions book over there to see if the marketers or those well-to-do doctors are doing your jobs. Most times, he just stares at us, shakes his head and goes back to his office and watch the stock markets. Abe, stop worrying about my team, you're not the CEO! Now, get out of my office. Stephanie, call security!"

Oh my God, if the CEO was a fly on the wall he would've seen and heard it for himself why his business office employees exhibit an "unprofessional attitude" and their customer service is so atrocious! But to think of it, if he was a fly on the wall the employees that don't pick up the telephone would pick up a fly swatter and kill the fly or the CEO before he can do anything about the information he just gathered.

Chapter 6

THE EMPLOYEES

IN 2001, THERE WERE OVER 100 million employees working in America. Urban Community Hospital had over 250 employees and there were two types: the functional employees and the dysfunctional employees. The functional employees had been employed by the hospital for three years or more, which meant that they usually had an invisible pass to do whatever they wanted to do, when they wanted to do it, and at times without any repercussions. They presented themselves as the normal employees who appeared to be dedicated, caring, and committed to their jobs, the customers and for providing excellent service. They were likable, developed positive relationships, followed the rules, avoided unnecessary conflicts, participated in teamwork, and elevated their job performances. They also celebrated the hospitals mission, by helping every customer, working hard and enlarging the hospital's brand, vision and the bottom line.

The dysfunctional employees were the individuals we had to tolerate by being forced to work with. They rejected change, resisted common sense principles, were not professional, and unable to control their harmful emotions. They never followed the hospital's policies, and were not committed to serving the customers with quality, excellence, and the needed services, they deserved. They wouldn't correct their destructive behavior if Dr. Phil was their supervisor. I used to wonder why a dysfunctional employee would work for a medical hospital, particularly since they didn't care about the patients, their health, wellness, and outcomes. They were paid for 80 hours of work like every other employee and wouldn't embrace and implement the hospital's mission, ethics, and standards. They should've been fired or quit a long time ago. They should have exited to go work for the worst prison system on the planet and tormented their most vicious criminals like they tortured us.

At times it seemed like the administrators of the hospital were giving the dysfunctional employees the green light to unleash their abnormal actions, which dispirited the functional employees who strived to be professional, positive, and productive. Their behavior minimized the standards of quality, kindness, and care, which was destroying morale, teamwork, and our professional culture. The functional employees wanted to quit their jobs on the patients, the hospital, and community they served. Many of them gave up.

The dysfunctional employees more than likely became dysfunctional because of their history, childhood, family, social status, and multiplicity of personal problems, which were unknown to others. You never knew what an employee was going through in their life, world and experiences. They came to work every day, but were living with their own personal issues such as divorce, domestic violence, drugs, alcohol, death, gambling addictions, sexual harassment, home foreclosures, massive debt, bankruptcy, and medical and mental health challenges, which to others, seemed normal. They were one mistake away from getting fired, having a nervous breakdown, going postal, committing suicide, assaulting a co-worker, being admitted into a psychiatric hospital, or joining a terrorist group. I felt sorry for the dysfunctional employees, but especially the functional employees who had to work with them. They should have been protected, given free mental health therapy, allowed to have four weeks of paid vacation and a cash bonus.

Urban Community Hospital had an Employee Assistance Program (EAP) for those employees who needed help with their personal issues. It was a confidential program that provided the employees with a hot-line telephone number and the opportunity to schedule an appointment to talk with an external EAP counselor about their problems. The employees never used it because the dysfunctional environment became a part of the job. The director of the Human Resources (HR) department was Esther Thompson, who was a short, big-boned woman with bright red hair and looked a little like Lucille Ball, the comedian and TV star. Esther didn't present herself like the Director of HR. She dressed like every day was casual Fridays. When the hospital had an open house, tours and celebrations she was never introduced to the guests or VIP's because of her shoddy style. She was in charge of the employee's health benefits which included a free dental plan, but never utilized it.

> The employees never used the EAP because the dysfunctional environment became a part of the job.

Esther worked for the hospital for 14 years and didn't have a college degree. She didn't demonstrate any leadership skills, passion, or a strong work ethic. One of her responsibilities was to coordinate and execute the hospital's employee orientations, but presented them when she felt like it or a hospital manager demanded one for their new employees.

Esther's role as the Director of HR was not respected like most hospitals and companies. She wasn't allowed to interview, hire, reprimand, or fire employees, which was Mr. Doolittle's job. She collected the employees' timesheets and passed out their pay checks every other Friday, which made her feel like a boss. She was another one of the leading gossipers on the hospital's gossip team and had no shame in her game when it came to talking about another employee's personal life, dealings and salary. If Esther ever wrote a book about our crazy hospital and employees, it would be a #1 best-seller and if they made it into a Hollywood movie, she'll be an instant Billionaire.

Every month the hospital's managers had to attend a mandatory meeting to discuss hospital business, and Mr. Doolittle always chaired the meeting. One month he reminded all the managers to schedule their employees and themselves to attend the hospital's first ever customer service training, and wanted me to inform everyone about it.

Mr. Doolittle was setting up the customer service training by saying that, "One of the problems that our hospital is facing is unsatisfactory customer service. We have designed a customer service training that is mandatory for all employees to attend. Abe will facilitate the workshops for every employee, including the doctors. Abe, tell the managers a little bit about the training."

"Thank you Mr. Doolittle. The hospital's customer service training is entitled 'The Prescriptions for Impeccable Customer Service!' The goal is to teach every employee how to provide excellent customer service and what it will do to increase the hospital's services, reputation, and patient care. I read a quote from my phone and the writer who was anonymous stated that, 'Customer service is the lifeblood of any organization. Everything flows from it and nourished by it. Customer service is not a department...it's an attitude.' I really believe that if we as a team, and a family would renew our attitudes, we can renew our thinking, behavior, actions and the future of a hospital we all love and every patient needs."

Tonia asked, "Abe, when are the workshops? I hope they're not on Mondays. My employees don't come to work on the Mondays after payday!"

"We're scheduling them for next month. Here's the sign-up sheets and when they're completed, please put them in my mailbox."

Urban Community Hospital didn't have an email system for employees. The CEO was taking his time on releasing the finances for the new computer system. He knew the hospital needed it, but wanted the employees to be working and not sitting around playing games on their computers and emailing each other unnecessarily.

Bernie Jakes, who was the Chief Financial Officer of the hospital, asked, "Abe, will all the senior administrators and doctors participate in the customer service trainings? We should all be leading by example."

"Bernie, as you know it's everyone's responsibility, from the CEO to the valet team who park the cars. We need to teach every employee the customer service principles, and give them the tools and strategies on how to implement impeccable customer service. I truly believe that if we put our customer service skills into action, it'll take this hospital to a new dimension. Thank you!"

After the meeting Bernie hung around and asked me another question. "Abe, you do know why the employee's work at Urban Community, don't you? It's not because of your doggedness to teach them how to improve their customer service skills; it's to get paid. Tell them that if they don't provide impeccable customer service to our patients who really pay their salaries, they will not get paid and watch our customer service sky rocket out the building."

Bernie Jakes was the leader of Urban Community's Finance Department which was the hospital's treasury department. His responsibilities were to supervise and manage the hospital's accounting, billing, and the business departments. He was also responsible for managing the outside medical clinics. Bernie was a want to be cheaper version of Warren Buffet, who invested in high returns, cut unnecessary expenses, supervised budgets, eliminated business contracts, and kept the hospital in the black. He made sure the CEO's bank accounts looked like Bank of America. He was around 5'6, obese, and a relentless money maker for the hospital. If the CEO and the doctors were multi-millionaires, he was in the top ten. Every now and then I would ask him how the hospital was doing and he would say, "I'm still here aren't I?"

Urban Community Hospital employed hundreds of employees and had eighteen departments throughout the hospital. The majority of the employees who worked in the Housekeeping and Maintenance Department, Dietary, Laboratory, Pharmacy, Radiology, Finances, Social Services, Human Resources, Marketing, Emergency Room, Information Technology, Security, Medical Records, Quality Improvement, Nursing, Transportation, and Physical Therapy department attended the customer service trainings.

The doctors, administrators and managers also attended the trainings and were motivated to make sure that the employees practiced and modeled what they learned. Once each employee left the Customer Service Training they received a customer service guide, lapel pen, and copy of the pledge.

The pledge declared: "To put the patients first, exhibit a positive attitude, communicate with everyone, work as a team, implement excellence in care, provide quality programs and services, exceed the customers' expectations, and be the best customer service provider in healthcare!" That's what everyone promised.

Summer who worked in the nursing department and one of the participants congratulated me and whispered, "Excellent job Abe, keep the faith and always remember that all things are possible to the one who believes."

Chapter 7

THE DOCTORS

HEALTHCARE IS AN EXTREMELY COMPETITIVE industry for every hospital in America, and to be profitable they need to hire the best specialized, primary care, and patient friendly doctors, possible. Doctors are not only tremendously successful, but in high demand. They play a vital role on a hospital's medical team by escalating and elevating the mission, vision, image, patients, revenue, and community it serves.

If you want to have money for life, be a doctor. I grew up watching a lot of superhero movies and television shows, but the real superheroes from my perception are the doctors who are committed to saving lives. Why would an exceptional doctor, who had privileges at two or three flourishing hospitals, want to practice medicine for a hospital in the middle of the hood? Money!

At Urban Community Hospital, the doctors were required to bring their own patients with them, but usually didn't. They referred and admitted their patients to their preferred hospitals. The doctors who worked for us received new patients, treated assigned patients, sat around the nursing stations, gossiped and flirted with the employees, communicated on their smart phones, watched free cable TV, read the *Wall Street Journal*, took power naps, and got paid every two weeks like every other employee, unless they had other arrangements.

Most hospitals had a shortage of specialized and primary care doctors who were difficult to recruit, hire, and sustain. A good number of them seemed arrogant, narcissistic and almost certainly thought they had been blessed with the same life-saving and healing powers as Jesus Christ. They healed the sick, raised the dead, gave vision to the blind, and made medical miracles happen in the palms of their hands. I've learned from years of experience that God works through people, prayer, faith, action and in mysterious ways.

> The health-care industry was starting to evolve with a new generation of patients who aspired to be their own personal doctors.

The healthcare industry was starting to evolve with a new generation of patients who aspired to be their own personal doctors. They read up-to-the-minute medical books, health magazines and gathered medical information from the experts on the internet to learn everything they could about preventative health, their medical conditions, and symptoms, to make their own medical diagnosis.

The new generation of patient doctors believed they could heal themselves, save money, and avoid expensive medical procedures, control their cost and bills. They purchased their medications faster online, at low cost, with unbelievable faith, and practiced medicine on themselves which not only healed their minds and bodies, but finances. They knew what a lot of patients or consumers didn't know, that the main reason why people file for bankruptcy is medical expenses.

The doctors at Urban Community Hospital were licensed medical physicians who had graduated from a prestigious medical school, and worked for years as a hospital intern to become the specialist in their field of medicine. They swore to uphold the sacred "Hippocratic Oath," which is taken by licensed physicians, who swore by a number of healing Gods, to uphold specific ethical standards and provide the best quality services possible.

One day, Mr. Doolittle asked me to be the master of ceremony for an awards dinner for the hospital's medical doctors at a five-star restaurant in the Gold Coast area of Chicago. The hospital was presenting Dr. Michael Gold, the Medical Director, with the doctors Heroes award for his undying care, dedication, and service to the hospital for over 23 years. Dr. Gold was a multi-millionaire and one of the specialized doctors employed at three of the finest hospitals in Chicago and the suburbs. He was known as the Pied Piper of medicine and wherever he went, his patients followed.

Nearly most of the hospital's physicians attended – socializing, eating gargantuan steaks, lobsters and sushi, gulping on the top shelf liquor, and bragging energetically about their success stories. The hospital only had one African American physician, and he was a no show, which made me feel like the legendary Sammy Davis Jr. hanging out with the rat pack.

Dr. Gold was responsible for the success of the psychiatric and drug and alcohol treatment units. The nurses who worked on the units resented him; they accused him of acting like an emperor who could be very condescending. Let's just say that he was the Godfather of doctors, and made the nurses offers they couldn't refuse. If the nurses and other employees didn't treat his patient's with the kindness, respect, and care they deserved, he stopped admitting them and transferred them to a hospital that would.

Dr. Tony Valentine was another physician in attendance. He reminded me of those TV doctors who were tall, tanned, and handsome, with a head full of good-looking silver hair, and a top patient admitter for the hospital. Dr. Valentine was married with five children and known as the ladies' man. Other than being one of the top medical surgeons at Urban Community Hospital, his other area of expertise was dating stunning nurses. His newest girlfriend's name was Malaysia, and she was young, single, and breathtaking, but didn't take any mess. She became one of his championship trophies. The gossip wire said that they were having hot sex wherever there were no hospital cameras. Most of them were out of order.

One evening Malaysia visited Dr. Valentine's off-site office to meet him, but spied on him. She sat in her luxury car for hours until he exited. He departed with another attractive female, who wasn't his wife. After they strolled to their cars holding hands, they kissed and she drove off. He danced to his truck and went into shock! His brand new luxury truck was ruined! The windows were broken out, leather seats sliced up, all four tires were flat, and derogatory graffiti was written everywhere.

A week later Malaysia marched into a doctor's only meeting and threw her "Malaysia Secrets" lingerie which Dr. Valentine bought her into his lap. The other doctors and CEO were stunned and enraged, and the CEO threatened to fire Malaysia, but Dr. Valentine begged him not to. He promised to give her some medication to cope with her withdrawals.

Another doctor at the awards dinner was Dr. Marcus Murdock, who was another specialized surgeon and respected by his colleagues and the hospital employees. If you weren't a patient of his and needed a prescription for anything, he'd happily write you one. He was a favorite of the male employees because he wrote them a prescription for the wonder pill that transformed them from a two-minute man into an Ironman. Dr. Murdock was assigned to work in the hospital's emergency room, and after treating the patients they would follow up with him at one of his outside medical clinics for medical treatments, which usually required some type of surgery. His get rich by any means necessary schemes consisted of complex surgeries for as many patients as possible, even if they didn't need them.

Several years ago the politicians, community activists, and social service providers in the community took action against Dr. Murdock. They wrote letters to the states medical board, law enforcement and other politicians about him, facilitated town hall meetings, and interacted with the media to get his medical license revoked, with no results. They accused him of being a 21st century slave master and the patients were his so-called slaves. History says a "slave" is a person who is entirely under the power or influence of another person, place or thing. The criticisms were that some of his patients appeared locked up in a mental, physical, and medical bondage. Dr. Murdock intentionally allowed his patients to remain in poor health so they had to keep visiting him for their medical treatment and needless surgeries, to bill the state's Medicare and Medicaid programs for his medical services.

A good number of people in the communities were uneducated, unemployed, and had been incarcerated. To survive, a few of them appeared to manipulate the healthcare system by paying a doctor a fee to sign the paperwork and provide them with a bogus mental health medical diagnosis to qualify for Medicare and Medicaid benefits.

Once a person was admitted into the hospital for a mental health disorder, they received psychotropic drugs, a room and bed, three meals a day with snacks, cigarettes, and an all-inclusive vacation from their outside responsibilities. The person would be calculated as a hospital admission and so-called "slave" to their mental diagnosis, physician, the healthcare system, and unfortunately for the rest of their lives. If Harriet Tubman was alive today, she'll say it's time to free the slaves.

Once the award dinner was over most of the doctors took a cab home to avoid a DUI. When the doctors at Urban Community

Hospital arrived to work, they walked around like royalty. Once the patients saw their doctors on the medical floors, wearing their white lab coats and stethoscopes around their neck, they illuminated like Christmas lights. The patients really believed that they were receiving the best medical treatment and services possible.

A few of the doctors at Urban Community were committed and strived to be their best, which elevated their profession. They treated the patients as human beings, and not numbers. They provided the patients with compassion, enthusiasm, and quality service, in spite of their ethnicity, physical disability, age or sexual orientation, educational and economic backgrounds, diversified languages, and zip codes.

The best doctors were treated with high regard and celebrated by their colleagues, the families, and communities, and, of course, the patients. They treated every patient as if God referred them personally. The doctors who are unquestionably the best figured it out a long time ago – if they didn't heal the patients, who else would?

Chapter 8

THE NURSES

"ABE, DID YOU HEAR ABOUT DAVE?" exclaimed Esther, the Director of Human Resources running into my office. Esther was a little out of shape, so I was shocked to see her running.

"No, what happened?"

"The hospital's maintenance men Justin and Marcus told the CEO and Mr. Doolittle that Dave was sexually harassing them. They said that he was cracking derogatory jokes, touching them inappropriately and buying tickets to sporting events. He was begging them to go out to lunch, dinner, cocktails, and a motel."

With a moment of confusion, I responded, "Sexual Harassment? You're talking about Dave Hardaway, the Vice President of Nursing? He's a married man with two kids!"

Esther sat down, shaking her head, neck and hands, and quickly replied, "Don't be naïve. The married men I know are the biggest super freaks on the planet. That's why I'm not married. The CEO has been trying to get some dirt on Dave for years. The administrators asked him to meet them at the hospital's lawyer's office to talk about another employee and told him Donald Trump's favorite words – You're fired!"

"Dave was in the big boys' club! They probably allowed him to resign and gave him a separation agreement with a huge severance package on his way out the door."

Esther started laughing and said, "If it was any other employee they would've escorted their butts out of the hospital faster than the rats that runs out of my office every morning."

"The rat's snacks are in your office. What is the Nursing Department going to do now?"

"They already hired someone! We had over two hundred people applying for the job."

"You know what they say, everybody wants a job, but everybody doesn't want to work."

Once the storm was over and the gossip wire stopped chatting about Dave, it was time for me to visit the Nursing Department. I spoke with their administrative assistant, Summer, who was an unapologetic Christian woman who wore fashionable bi-focal glasses and could see a sinner coming twenty-six miles away. She was amazingly wise and attractive for her age and always happy in spite of a speech disorder. She worked for the hospital for over 12 years and had a daily scripture waiting to share with any co-worker who needed encouragement.

"Summer, how's the Good life?"

"Abe, the Good life is the God life and it's outstanding. God's still in the blessing business, so get blessed by the best, and join the God squad."

"Did you go to church Sunday?"

"I attend church every Sunday and twice during the week. My relationship with God helps me fight the haters in this unpredictable world. Haters are everywhere, but when you know who you are and whose you are, you can transform the haters into your motivators, educators and elevators. No weapon formed against his children shall prosper, because we're more than conquerors!"

Every time I talked to Summer she made me want to repent. I thought about asking her out for dinner, but was afraid she might throw a little holy water on me.

I laughed to myself and asked her, "What's the word for today?"

Summer's eyes lit up as she replied, 'Seek ye first the kingdom of God and His righteousness and all things shall be added unto you.'

Abe asked, "Is your new boss in?"

"God is my boss and he's always in. He's in my heart, mind and spirit. The new nursing administrator is in her office. Abe, never forget, God is our spiritual daddy and he's always watching you."

"I hope he's watching our co-workers, too. Look, if I'm not out of her office in ten minutes, call 911."

I knocked on the office door to introduce myself to the new Vice President of Nursing. Her name was Jackie Hogan, and she was brawny looking, in her early forties, with a hair style that resembled an elementary school football coach. It was ten below zero outside, and she wore a Hawaiian shirt with a pack of cigarettes in her pocket. I enthusiastically introduced myself and welcomed Jackie to the hospital, informing her that if she needed anything from the marketing department, she should contact me. I really didn't know what was up with the nurses' new supervisor, but she was looking at me like I was planning to snatch her purse.

A nurse's commitment, passion, and contributions to a hospital are irreplaceable.

Urban Community Hospital, like every hospital in America, could not survive without their registered and licensed practical nurses. A nurse's commitment, passion, and contributions to a hospital are irreplaceable. Jackie was hired to restructure the hospital's nursing department and put the nurses back to work. The CEO viewed the nurses at his hospital as lazy, incompetent, not patient-friendly, and overpaid. However, if you quizzed those same nurses, most of them would say that they were unappreciated, understaffed, and under paid.

The nurses were responsible for taking care of the patients, monitoring their vital signs, distributing medications, charting on them and communicating with the doctors, hospital employees, and family members. Jackie's assignment was to transform the nursing culture, get rid of the difficult nurses, and recruit better ones, and teach them how to reach higher heights in their profession.

I believe the hospital fired Dave, the former VP of Nursing, not because of the sexual allegations against him, but because of his lack of leadership, accountability, and effectiveness in managing his nurses and the department. Dave allowed the nurses to get away with murder. They screamed at each other during meetings, took long lunch breaks, refused to wear their orange scrubs, didn't want to work as a team and were disrespectful to the doctors and patients. Dave was too soft to be a boss.

The hospital needed Jackie to be the leader and guide the Nursing Department into the 21st century, but to everyone's surprise, including myself, the hospital administrators hired Lucifer's baby sister. She became the nurse from hell and put the fear of insecurity in all of her nurses. She had a license to bully. She confronted the nurses on the medical units, in patients' rooms, and once she had one of them in her office for an interrogation, it became a verbal wrestling match.

Jackie had a bad habit of putting her hand in their face, cursing them out, belittling them, and making abusive remarks. She would lie on them and wrote them up for trivial things. She took pleasure in messing with a nurse's mind, obliterating their confidence, decreasing their pay checks, and trying to fire them. She was known to throw a nurse under the bus and would run over them driving eighty-five miles an hour. Some of the nurses hated her guts and the ones who chose to stay and work for the hospital learned how to endure her wrath because their income depended on it.

The gossip wire said that she cursed out a male nurse on the unit and he cried like a four-year old. He ran away from his good paying job and never came back.

Jackie's outdated leadership tactics, argumentative personality, and unpredictable behavior created a hostile working environment for the nurses. Three of the celebrated Asian nurses filed discrimination and retaliation lawsuits against her. When they went to court the judge suggested that the CEO and the hospital's lawyers fire her, or get ready for more lawsuits. The lawsuits were settled out of court and Jackie never retreated, she became more vindictive.

The nurses and employees finally realized that the craziest nurse administrator in healthcare worked at Urban Community Hospital. I used to wonder what would happen if the security guards had to take Jackie down, who would end up in the emergency room.

Chapter 9

THE SENIORS

"ABE HAVE YOU HEARD?" Esther shouted! "Helen's taking over for America in the Seniors for Life Program."

"Helen doesn't have a GED!" I said, and Esther left me confused.

Urban Community Hospital had a Senior Program and it was advertised as a "Locally Recognized" senior citizen program in Chicago. America Rodriquez, the Vice President of Geriatrics, created the program in her basement. The senior patients worshipped the ground she walked on. She treated every one of them with the upmost care, respect, and like family. America was *Vogue* magazine beautiful, highly educated, a hands-on leader, and wore white dresses and pant suits during the winter seasons. She gracefully stopped and talked to the patients when she walked around the center and throughout the hospital. She was known for comforting patients by holding their hands when they visited with the doctors. The patients, doctors, and employees valued her energy, compassion, and work ethic.

America took great joy in complimenting and supporting the hospital employees when they performed exceptional duties for the patients. It was her idea to create an employee's committee to vote and choose an employee of the month and year. The employee of the year was always the main event and handed out at the hospital's annual holiday party. One month, I won the employee of the month award, and, of course, the haters said it was a sham.

America was the only administrator that could keep the CEO and Mr. Doolittle in their place. When they would try to get away with not spending money on hospital improvements, medical equipment, or patient services, she made sure the hospital always had what was needed. She tried to persuade the CEO not to hire Jackie as the VP of Nursing, but was muted. I had the upmost respect for America because she was a leader who led by example, with courage and an empathetic spirit.

One day, while meeting with America (smiling proudly), she said, "Senor Abe, you're the best marketer Mr. Doolittle has ever hired and better than the reps on my marketing team."

America was the best leader I've ever known ... she knew the secret to building positive relationships.

"Thank you, America! You know what they say, you're the Jennifer Lopez of what you do, and I'm the Michael Jordan of what I do!"

"Jennifer Lopez? No disrespect to my girl from the block, but I'm the Oprah Winfrey of what I do! Nobody cares more about the patients more than me. I give them stuff, everyday. Abe, how old do you think I am? Don't answer that! I'm 40 something but look and feel like I'm still in my twenties. It's ok to look, but don't stare, and please don't touch or I'll have to cut you like a porterhouse steak. I'm joking with your cute self. Abe, may I ask how old are you and do you have a lady?"

"I'm ageless, fearless and priceless! Yes I have a lady!"

"Great answer. Just remember that no matter your age or who you're with; never give up on your dreams, your passion, your health, and your purpose."

America was the best leader I've ever known and always had something encouraging to say to an employee because she knew the secret to building positive relationships.

Urban Community Hospital's Senior Center had their own marketers and kept the hospital flowing with patients. They loved serving seniors. They smiled, laughed, had fun, and worked hard. They were indispensable and one big happy family. It was because of America's leadership style that her team always gave 1,000% and raised the bar to excellence, quality and customer service and hospital admissions.

One day, America vanished without a trace. The administrators kept things on the down low, but the gossip wire told everybody that she had to go downtown and meet with the hospital's lawyers, and was never seen or heard from again. The new VP of Geriatrics for the hospital and Senior Center became Helen Parker. America hired her as a marketer and was her mentor. Helen was tall, curvy, dressed like a school principal, and had that "stab you in the back" type of personality. It was time for me to trade in my bullet proof vest for a stainless steel blazer.

The administrators had faith that Helen could duplicate America's success with the Senior Center. Her mission was to bring in more seniors with Medicare, Medicaid, and private insurance and after several months of hard work, she became the new queen of senior care.

After Helen started having some surprising success, her promotion, new power, and increase in income elevated her oversized ego. She stopped working and began shouting orders to the center's employees to keep the patients that America's marketing team had previously brought in. The seniors remained constant until Helen fired her marketers and brought in her own team. Eventually, she became devious, demanding, and manipulative.

Helen's mandate to her new marketers was to bring in 15 new senior patient admissions a month. Her team went above and beyond the call of duty, by typing her letters and memos, dropping off and picking up her laundry from the cleaners, baby sitting her daughter in the office, and keeping her Range Rover cleaned and detailed daily. In spite of all the personalized assignments she gave them, they still had to market the program and achieve their monthly quotas or face the unhappiness of unemployment.

The senior medical center started losing patients to the new senior competition and its clinics. Helen assumed the seniors would remain loyal, but was clueless to the mission of the new competition, which was to win market share. She never implemented any new ideas to increase new territories, patient admissions, and revenue. The new marketers couldn't flip the script and the doctors became disappointed.

Urban Community's administrators fell asleep at the wheel, and the competition was driving like the *Fast and the Furious* to reach their goals. They must have stolen our blueprint on senior services and was taking it to a customer friendly level. They were providing the seniors with better doctors, marketers and employees, beautiful surroundings, state-of-the-art medical equipment, free transportation, interactive social activities, catered lunches and gave them beautiful plants to take home.

I wondered what America would do?

Chapter 10

THE PSYCHIATRIC UNIT

WHO COULD HAVE REALIZED that the employees who worked for Urban Community Hospital had just as many problems as the patients they served? Most of them experienced their own psychological problems and still worked. No matter what were their unknown psychotic, neurotic and physical problems, they still had to exhibit professionalism, compassion, accountability, and productivity in the workplace.

The patients admitted into our hospital's psychiatric unit were diagnosed with a mental illness disorder, which had to be paid for by Medicaid, Medicare, and their private insurance provider. No medical benefits, no mental health services. The charges were for their room, board, counseling, and prescription medications.

The mental health community has an informational book called the DSM (Diagnostic and Statistical Manual of Mental Disorders), which is utilized by mental health professionals to gather critical research about psychiatric disorders and the definitions of symptoms. When I used to work in the mental health field, the DSM book was also known as the mental health bible which listed all of the psychiatric diagnoses, like schizophrenia, bipolar disorders, major depressive disorders, social anxiety disorders, and other acceptable mental disorders that can be used to treat and admit a person into a mental health hospital.

The mental health bible stated that, "Mental disorders may start in the mind, but can become physical disorders." They are so common in the United States that statistics report that one in five Americans have a diagnosable mental disorder each year. This includes 44 million adults and 13.7 million children. Mental illness that's untreated can be as disabling as heart disease or cancer in terms of premature death and lost productivity. Mental illness should not be stigmatized and trivialized because it can interfere with the quality of a person's precious life, assets, and can cause unnecessary pain, suffering, and alienation.

Urban Community Hospital's psychiatric unit was isolated on the fifth floor. The majority of the employees who didn't work on the unit were always afraid to visit because of the mentally ill patients. They were probably afraid because the unit's clinical team could diagnose them just by sitting down and listening to all the abnormal things that happens in their personal life.

The psychiatric unit was secured and the doors were always locked and needed a key to get through, or you had to be buzzed in by the employees. The unit had 40 beds, carpeted floors, and was a dark, chilly and unfriendly place to be. The heating system didn't always work during the winter season and in the summer the air conditioning was constantly out of order. The unit had an awful odor. The housekeepers said they couldn't locate the smell, but I would have bet anyone, that if their supervisor placed a $100 bill next to the smell, they would have found it in seconds.

The patients on the unit appeared disoriented, over medicated, and always talking to themselves, pacing up and down the halls (their butts exposed from wearing those cut-rate dark blue hospital gowns) like they were on a conveyor belt. They watched the unit door open and close, to see who they could annoy and seemed to get pleasure from it. If the door didn't close properly, it didn't matter; they were too sapped to make a run for it.

When Dr. Gold, the patients' doctor, arrived on the unit to make his rounds, they surrounded him as if he was a rock star.

Most of them wanted to get discharged, have their medications changed, and receive double portions of food or a judgmental employee fired.

The day shift was usually quiet; their employees (nurses, mental health counselors, other doctors, and social workers) were usually on top of their duties. The evening and midnight shifts were when the real party started. That's when the employees let the patients do whatever they wanted to do, except kill someone. The counselors who worked on the evening shift were twin brothers named Joey and Jerry. They looked like they could have played for the Chicago Bears fourth string team. They had a great sense of humor, always joking, laughing, very energetic, and always starving. When they were on duty, the employees knew who were going to make the food run.

The female patients (when mentally healthy were attractive women) on the unit had serious psychological problems, but the gossip wire said that the twins were having inappropriate relationships with them. The psychiatric unit became their personal players club, and every time the supervisors needed someone to work overtime, they asked the twins. Everyone thought they wanted to work to make some extra money, but were feeding their lustful misdeeds and extracurricular activities. They never had to worry about the evening or midnight shift's supervisors making rounds and interrupting their little escapades, because like most of the patients, they were asleep too.

It was shocking to fathom the twins performing indecent activities with the female patients. One day a couple of the female patients were admitted back into the hospital and after a few days they informed the unit employees about the unthinkable things that the twins had them doing for food, liquor, and cigarettes. The unit employees didn't believe the accusations and like everything else, tried to sweep them under the carpet. Maybe that was another reason why the unit smelled so bad? The unit employees didn't react to the female patients' repugnant stories until they informed their doctor. They told Dr. Gold everything and he listened to their every word on how they moved in with the twin's after being discharged from their last hospital admission. After the brief meeting, Dr. Gold became extremely concerned and furious, and communicated the female patients' unbelievable stories to the CEO and Mr. Doolittle. An emergency meeting was called and the female patients repeated their stories once again to their doctor, Mr. Doolittle, the nursing supervisor, and Captain Farmer, head of the security department.

The female patients revealed that the twin's devious plans were to meet them at a currency exchange around the corner from the hospital, pick them up in their black Tahoe, and take them to their apartment on the Southside. They roomed with the twins for weeks until they grew tired of them. When it was time for them to depart, they gave the female patients a few dollars each; bus passes, a pack of cheap cigarettes to share, and instructed them not to tell anyone about their little secrets. Mr. Doolittle advised the patients not to tell their stories to anyone else, until they investigated their serious accusations.

The twins were called into a separate meeting with Mr. Doolittle, Jackie, the Vice President of Nursing, the evening supervisors, and the head of security. Joey and Jerry denied everything. Mr. Doolittle instructed Captain Farmer to go with the twins to their apartment to check out a few details. He went and came back to the hospital and confirmed what the female patients had described about their apartment. Mr. Doolittle called a cell phone number that one of the female patients had given to him and one of the twins answered it. Mr. Doolittle and the other managers believed the female patients and fired the twins with the CEO's blessing. The female patients were banned from the hospital, but since they still had Medicare benefits, were transferred to another hospital, where Dr. Gold had privileges.

The number one rule in healthcare is to not have a personal relationship with a patient, especially female patients. How would the twins, doctors, hospital employees and administrators felt, if the female patients were their mother, wife, sister, niece, cousin, or daughter? We must give every patient the same respect that we would give our mothers. They say you reap what you sow, so the twins will get what they deserve. But what's going to happen to the care givers who keep letting the patients down? What's going to happen to the female patients? My prayers to God was to forgive all of us and teach everyone how to "do the right thing" before it's too late.

Chapter 11

THE DRUG TREATMENT PROGRAM

URBAN COMMUNITY HOSPITAL operated a very lucrative Drug and Alcohol Treatment program that was originally created to stop the drugs and alcohol addictions that were plaguing the community. The hospital's goal was to develop a Drug Treatment program to help people with their chemical dependency problems and provide them with the opportunity to make a full recovery and live a better life.

There were four levels of care for a person who wanted to make a life-saving decision, to live a drug and alcohol free life.

- The first level of care is a Medical Detoxification Program, which is designed to eliminate the drugs and alcohol from the body of a chemically dependent person with or without the use of other drugs. When a person medically detox from their drug of choice, they experience withdrawals, which can be dangerous, and should only be attempted under medical supervision.

- The second level of care is an Inpatient Residential Rehabilitation Treatment Program, which is designed to provide a person treatment that has gone through medical detox and is sober and drug free. This level of treatment will help them on their journey to recovery. The inpatient program will provide a person with at least ten to thirty days of treatment (whatever their health care benefits allow), a personalized treatment plan, group counseling, one on one individual therapy, and an introduction to the twelve step self-help program.

- The third level of care is an Intensive Outpatient Treatment Program, which consists of the same structure of treatment and care that a person needs, but on an outpatient basis. The advantage is that the patients learn how to stay clean and sober in the real world, rather than in the sheltered world of an inpatient facility.

- The fourth level of care is an Aftercare Treatment Program, which is designed to provide a person with a counselor, and a recovery plan of action that will teach them the importance of participating in the twelve step program and attending meetings such as AA (Alcoholic Anonymous), NA (Narcotic Anonymous) and GA (Gambling Anonymous). The recovery plan of action will provide them with an inspirational support system to teach them how to develop a personal relationship with their higher power.

Urban Community Hospital provided only one level of care for their patients, which was level one, the Medical Detox program, but had the resources to refer someone to other levels of care. If a potential patient didn't have Medicaid or private insurance they were referred to a government funded program, which usually had a very long waiting list.

What differentiated our Medical Detox program from the competitions was that the doctor provided his patients with the drug Suboxone (A combination of Buprenorphine and the anti-overdose drug Naloxone), and not methadone as the prescribed medication to detox the patients with an Opioid-use disorder.

Like methadone, Suboxone prevented drug sickness and reduced the cravings, without getting an addict high. It was determined by the National Institute on Drug Abuse that it was the gold standard for heroin addicts in medication assisted treatment.

One day, an overly animated patient said to me, "Mr. Washington thanks for sending the van to pick me up. I hope I don't have to wait too long to get some help."

I enthusiastically said, "My brother, my brother I'm so glad you made it. They say that the steps of a good man are ordered by the lord. It's time to change your old habits into new habits, so you can reinvent your future. Let me call the drug treatment unit, so a counselor can come down here and get you registered. You know the process, to draw your blood, pee in a cup and before you start noggin off that heroin, we'll go to the cafeteria and get you something to eat.

"The patient who was very appreciative said, "Man, you know how to treat your patients."

I laughed it off.

"Stay encouraged and I'll see you later."

The Drug Treatment program was one of the hospital's major revenue generators and kept us in the black. When the competition wasn't doing well, our Drug Treatment program was making money every day, which equaled to millions of dollars each year. The patients would detox for three days, and after they discharged from us, they could come back in a few days, three or four times a month. One day during supervision with Mr. Doolittle, we discussed new ideas on how I could increase my marketing efforts to gain more awareness, to admit more patients.

"Abe, I need you to do me a favor. If you can double your quota from 20 patients a month to 40, I will increase your bonus to an extra $3,000 a quarter."

"How can I say no to you, Mr. Doolittle? Can you please put that in writing for me?"

"Please don't quote me, but the government says, it's illegal to pay marketers a bonus for bringing in individual patient admissions, but only for revenue generated. We'll write something up and I'll sign it, and let's keep it between us."

"Mr. Doolittle is it okay if I put a big banner on the fence outside the hospital, to start promoting the Drug Treatment program to the potential customers and family members who drive by the hospital every day?"

"Abe, you don't have to tell me what you're going to do, just get results."

Once the Drug Treatment program's census started to sky rocket to a higher level, the employees who worked on the unit with the patients felt overwhelmed, and became stressed out, lazy and disrespectful with the patients. They were unprofessional and refused to answer the telephones in a timely manner, which caused the hospital to lose potential patients. If the Drug Treatment program had a big increase of new patients for a few months in a row, the employees would slack off, and the following months our patient admissions would decrease. The program employees really had it made because whenever we treated patients to pizza parties, free haircuts, and treats, the employees participated and enjoyed themselves too.

The Drug Treatment program supplied the patients with free cigarettes and the employees would not only smoke with the patients, but smoked for free and took a couple of packs home with them. Once the program employees became stressed out, they became temperamental. They put the patients on the ban list for any little itty bitty thing, just so they wouldn't come back and they didn't have to work.

The banned and unhappy patients would go back to their referral contacts, family members, and community culture and inform everyone that our Drug Treatment program and services were substandard. I talked to the program employees, and reminded them that no matter whom the patients were or where they came from, anything less than positive, caring, and professional service was a disservice. I disliked their unprofessional behavior and discussed it with my supervisor. He talked to Jackie, who was also the nursing director over the program about the problems, and she wouldn't move a muscle to improve the program and stop the employees from sabotaging our success.

One day I was called to Jackie's office.

"Mr. High Pants. Why do you always wear your pants up so high?"

I hated it when she called me that, but I quickly stated, "Jackie, boys wear their pants down below their waist, but real men wear their pants up high."

"Whatever, why do you go and run your big mouth off to Mr. Doolittle and tell him every single little thing that's going on in this hospital?" Jackie insultingly asked.

"What are you talking about, Jackie?"

"Mr. Doolittle told me about the little white lies you've been telling him regarding the employees on the Drug Treatment unit and how they're putting those dope fiends you call patients in their place."

"Jackie, it's like what Superman told Lois Lane, I don't lie! You need to reprimand and teach your employees how to treat our patients with the care, respect, and service they deserve. If this hospital was in the suburbs or on the North side, they'll treat the patients like the rich drug addicts?"

"Abe shut up! I said it once and I'll say it again and again, you're the hospitals snitch!"

"Jackie, I'm from the Westside and snitches get stitches in the hood. I'm not a snitch! I'm known as a hero to our patients and trying to make a difference against the drug epidemic. So call me a snitch if you want to, but don't call me the N-word, or say anything about my mother because one of us will be in the emergency room getting stitches!"

Of course, I quickly exited her office.

Most evenings when I drove home and thought about my job, I felt hypocritical. My co-workers and I were not seriously trying to help the patients overcome their addictive lifestyle. I was too busy trying to become the Steve Jobs of marketing and increase revenue. I told our patients what the recovery community tells a drug addict that's trying to stay clean and sober, to keep coming back! I told them to keep coming back, knowing that the employees would treat them like crap! Greediness made me a dysfunctional marketer.

One evening the Drug Treatment program admitted a patient to the unit named Paulie. He was a 23-year old male, dually-diagnosed, chemically dependent, and a paranoid schizophrenic. He was delusional, heard voices, and used street drugs to treat his symptoms rather than take care of what was causing them. He was also diagnosed with the big disease with the little name.

Paulie was supposed to be admitted to the psychiatric unit; however, we accepted him, so he could detox from his heroin addiction first. After three days of cleaning that garbage out of his body, we were going to transfer him to the Psychiatric unit. One evening the unit nurse refused to give Paulie his prescribed medications after begging for them.

Little Bobby, the program counselor was a dwarf, but could stand tall if a situation got out of hand. He was a former drug addict and one of his assignments was to assist the nurses with the patients. He instructed Paulie to go back into his room and they would take care of him later.

Paulie grew enraged.

"Why do I have to wait forever?" He asked. "Just give me my freaking medication so I can go back to freaking sleep!"

Little Bobby replied, "You better do what I told you or I'm going to knock your butt out!"

"I dare you to hit me, I'll own this hospital and where would you work then!"

Little Bobby angrily whispered, "Just give me 10 minutes and I'm going to put your freaking medication up your butt."

Paulie became even more enraged and went back to his room and poured a chemical over his gowns, which he stole off the housekeeper's cart. He ran back into the unit's dayroom where the patients were smoking, grabbed a cigarette from one of them, and tried to set himself and trash cans on fire. The patients ran out of the dayroom as if a blood-sucking zombie from the *Living Dead* was chasing them, screaming, "Paulie is going to kill everybody and burn this freaking hospital to the ground!"

The program employees called a code red and the security guards rushed to the unit and gang-tackled Paulie and dragged him to his bedroom, and threw him in the shower. After the mayhem was over a few of the patients told Little Bobby that Paulie was providing inappropriate favors to the male patients for cigarettes. The program employees and his social worker talked to him regarding his destructive behavior on the unit.

The nursing supervisor, social worker, and program counselor talked to the patients who were supposedly involved with Paulie and discovered the rumors were accurate. The program employees escorted all of the male patients to the hospital's laboratory and tested them for the big disease with the little name. The test results came back negative.

Later on that evening, the hospital discharged the two male patients that were involved with Paulie and instructed them not to come back to the Drug Treatment program for six months. They transferred Paulie by ambulance to a state funded hospital, heavily medicated.

The employees couldn't tell the other patients about Paulie's complex medical challenges. They were restricted by the HIPAA (Health Insurance Portability and Accountability Act) privacy laws.

Chapter 12

THE CONSULTANT

ONE SUPER BUSY AFTERNOON I was paged to Mr. Doolittle's office.

"Abe, this is Waldo Pinella," introduced Mr. Doolittle.

"Abe Alexander pleased to meet you."

"Waldo has been hired as a business consultant for the hospital and I want you to spend a few weeks with him. Take him out and show him around our little ghetto, I mean the hood, I'm sorry I meant the community. Introduce him to a few of your referral sources and educate him on why we're the #1 hospital in Chicago."

"Sure," I said. "Let me check my appointment book and I'll let you know when I'm available."

"Take your time, I'll be around," replied Waldo.

Urban Community Hospital hired Waldo Pinella as a Business Consultant to assist the hospital in solving a number of its internal and external problems. His mission was to eliminate unnecessary waste, find out who the lazy managers and employees were, cut unnecessary expenses, recruit new doctors, increase our Medicare, Medicaid and Private Insurance business, and elevate the hospital's brand.

Waldo was a large guy, not only in size, but with his administrative experience, influence, and ego. He was middle aged, and wore the "rich man" look-bald headed with hair around the sides and no facial hair. He reminded me of a younger Mr. Potter in the Christmas movie *It's A Wonderful Life!* The hospital's employees were worried about a new business consultant because he was an outsider and they didn't know who he was or his intentions. Waldo had the green light to visit every department, ask employees questions, and at times just sit back and observe everything. I added Waldo on my schedule, and it was Showtime!

"We'll take my car since I know the hood," I said. "We're going to go visit my network and a few doctors."

Waldo inquired, "Do you mind if I smoke?"

"I rather you didn't. You might get some of those hot ashes on my leather seats and that smell. How do you do it? I guess you haven't heard what the surgeon general said?"

"What can I say? I'm suicidal."

I thought to myself, if the new guy doesn't take care of his health, how can he help our hospital and the patients? We finally reached one of our destinations.

"Come on Waldo, let's go in here and I'll introduce you to the community's rainbow coalition."

We strolled into the Dorothy Mae Wiley Center, which was named after a great community teacher and a non-for-profit organization that provided housing, comprehensive programs and services for the elderly, abused women, and substance abusers. We met with Veronique Stevenson, the service coordinator for the facility and a big referral source for the hospitals. While giving us a tour of the facility, she communicated to us that her administrator despised Urban Community Hospital. She stated that a few of our employees were rude, unprofessional, and disrespectful to their clients. She said the customer service was disgraceful and the only reason her organization refers to the hospital was because of me.

I didn't know Veronique was going to be so explicit about our hospital, Waldo seemed stunned. I was indebted to her mainly because the complaints about our employees and services were well-timed.

Waldo and I traveled everywhere. We visited most of the community social service agencies, businesses, and medical clinics that referred to us. We met with a doctor who communicated to him about the dissatisfaction with the hospital's treatment of his patients. He stated that when his medical team refers patients, they return to him complaining about the hospital's long waits and disappointing service. We also met with a few ministers at the community churches and they weren't preaching our praises either. They said our doctors and nurses were not compassionate and always found a reason to keep admitting one of their church members for something as little as a cold, but they'll keep praying for us.

While riding in the car, Waldo asked me, "Did you plan to take me to see all your unhappy customers who were complaining about the hospital's services?"

"I had to Waldo! I listen to those customers' complaints all the time and need some help to resolve them!"

"What are the hospital's administrators doing about the unsatisfactory service and issues that the customers are experiencing?

"I facilitated a customer service training a few years ago and that was it! After a while, the employees went back to treating the customers like they were the enemy. So now that you know the truth, what are you going to do about it?"

Waldo was smiling with appreciation for letting him hang with me for a few weeks and stated, "I have to give the CEO a written report of my findings and hopefully we can make some changes. Enough about work, where's the soul food restaurant around here? I'm hungrier than those pit bulls we seen barking at us in that yard the other day."

I felt great about letting Waldo go out into the field with me. He might be the help I've been praying for.

After a few months, Waldo reported his findings to the CEO and he hired him to become the new Chief Vice President of the hospital, which made him second in command. He was responsible for the hospital's administrators, managers, and marketers. They had to report to him except Bernie, the Vice President of Finances.

I had to give Waldo some kudos; he was trying his best to restructure everything, which was re-energizing the employees. I was assigned to report to him and he said that we were going to be like salt and pepper and my eyes lit up like a Grand Slam Breakfast. The first person Waldo fired was Mr. Doolittle, the Administrative Vice President and the CEO's right hand man. Mr. Doolittle had been an employee for years, worked for the CEO's father, hired me, and provided employment for so many community employees. He was the glue that kept the hospital together, but over time he fell out of favor with the CEO. The gossip wire stated that he cost the hospital millions in contracts for outdated computers and medical equipment.

I felt sorry for Mr. Doolittle and will miss him tremendously, but if Waldo can take this hospital to a new level, eventually it will be a blessing in disguise.

Waldo became the man and the mandate was to implement a transformation immediately. His first line of attack was to take over Helen's senior medical center because they were not bringing in the patients and revenue, which was vital to the hospital's future success. Waldo promised the CEO that he would increase the Medicare, Medicaid, and insurance business in months. During my supervisory meetings with Waldo, he pressed me for new ideas to increase patient admissions, so he could take them to the CEO as if they were his own.

I came up with an idea to increase the Medicare business by creating a senior wellness program titled: "Seniors in Action." It was a motivational, educational, and interactive program that provided exercising, dancing, and workshops for seniors. I recruited a few outside instructors who volunteered their expertise. We didn't charge the senior buildings, (they wouldn't have paid us anyway) to make them think they were receiving the services free and we were giving back to their community.

> I came up with an idea to increase the Medicare business by creating a senior wellness program titled: "Seniors in Action."

Once a senior needed a hospital for their medical needs, guess who they would choose? Everyone loved the new senior initiatives, except Helen! She never had an innovative idea in her life, but was not about to let Waldo and myself take the senior center out from under her.

The new senior wellness program started increasing the hospital's Medicare business. Unfortunately, Helen's daily complaints to the CEO were that the new program interfered with her senior center results and the doctors were concerned about losing patients. Her marketing team or spies came back and told her how the seniors were bragging about the new program and of course she wasn't getting any credit for its success. Waldo made me close the new senior program down and to put my focus back on marketing the hospital and Drug Treatment program. We left the seniors enrolled in the program confused, brokenhearted, and disappointed.

Jackie, the VP of Nursing, refused to work with Waldo. She didn't trust him and the only person that could tell her anything was the CEO. Jackie didn't like change, and the last thing she thought about was the success of the hospital. The interactions between Waldo and Jackie made her more combative, confrontational, and unprofessional to the employees, nurses, and doctors, and she blamed everybody but the woman in the mirror for her actions.

Waldo was no match for Jackie's explosive conduct, and asked the CEO to intervene. He really needed Jackie's cooperation to achieve his goals and plans for the hospital. The CEO stayed out of their battles, to see who would win. I thought Waldo was a diamond, but was acting like a marshmallow. The CEO loved wearing diamonds and Jackie loved eating marshmallows.

One meeting, Waldo and I were discussing ideas, and he whispered, "Abe, if I can make this hospital more successful, I could use this as a model for my consulting business."

After a year on the job, Waldo looked tired, confused and appeared to be losing his focus, passion, and purpose. He walked around the hospital in a gloomy mood and at times stayed in his office. He was probably hiding from Jackie and the CEO.

During another one of our Monday morning supervisory meetings, Waldo angrily stated, "Abe! I get tired of the CEO walking into my office complaining about patient admissions and asking me stupid questions. 'Where's the new patients,' 'how many new doctors have you brought in,' or 'what's wrong with the incompetent managers the hospital hired?'

"What's happening with your consulting business?" I asked.

"Abe, this country's in a bottomless recession. This is the only job I have, so I got to make this work!"

Then Waldo became a hero. He fired Jackie. The employees wanted to march into her office and express their amusement by performing the electric slide on her desk. Her administrative assistant, Summer, reminded us that the Bible says you can't rejoice once the enemy finally gets what they deserve. I danced in the washroom, alone.

One day I had to inform Waldo about my yearly bonus that was due. It was my biggest year ever with patient admissions. His response was that the CEO and he had decided not to give me a bonus because it wasn't in writing. I almost slapped that lie back in his mouth. I pulled out my bonus plan and showed it to him, and it was signed, sealed, and approved by the CEO and my former supervisor, Mr. Doolittle. He still wasn't satisfied, so I gave him a mini speech on why he should seriously reconsider. I told him a few inspiration stories about the former and first African-American Mayor of Chicago Harold Washington, the President of South Africa Nelson Mandela, and a community difference maker named Nancy Jefferson. The next day he handed me a $4,000 bonus check. After the disappointing circumstances regarding my bonus, it made me lose respect for Waldo. He was supposed to be an administrator in charge, and thought we were developing a friendship, but over time he became like most of the past hospital leaders and managers: manipulative, narcissistic, and untrustworthy. He was working for the hospital for only one thing, a paycheck.

Urban Community Hospital only had one African-American doctor and his name was Dr. Jeremiah Bridgewater. He was a renowned orthopedic surgeon who owned several orthopedic centers throughout Chicago. I met him at a female friend's wedding and recruited him to help the hospital increase their patient relationships with the Latino and African American population.

Dr. Bridgewater always looked like he just stepped out of *GQ* magazine. He stood around 6'4 and looked like Will Smith, the award winning actor. His strengths were his passion for healthcare reform, healing his patients, and educating the communities he worked in. He worked for the hospital for three years and one day one of his enemies showed up and it was Waldo. When they were in physician meetings together, Waldo was always insulting, arguing, and disagreeing with Dr. Bridgewater regarding his proficiency and his medical practices. They worked together years ago at another hospital where Waldo was fired and blamed the doctor's group, where Dr. Bridgewater was in charge.

One summer, Urban Community Hospital's administrators revoked Dr. Bridgewater's medical privileges. He was not allowed to visit, see, or treat his patients at the hospital. After weeks of meetings with the administrators, Dr. Bridgewater hired an attorney, who was his sister's husband, and filed a lawsuit with the EEOC (Equal Employment Opportunity Commission) and Human Rights Commission for racial discrimination, retaliation and defamation of character. He felt that the hospital administrators, specifically Waldo, were practicing hi-tech racism against him, his patients, and the communities he served. I felt embarrassed and fed-up because our hospital's business was put on blast in front of the community, residents and patients we served. We were supposed to be smarter than that.

Dr. Bridgewater became the "light of hope" in a deprived, forgotten and violence infested community. He marched around the hospital with a big sign that read "Boycott Urban Community Hospital; they discriminate against Latino and African-American doctors, employees and patients." He was a one-man protest and marched alone for one week. His weapons of mass destruction were his courage, faith, and a mega-phone. The next week, over 100 citizens joined his protest with their own signs marching like soldiers. The protest became the lead story on the 10 o'clock news and on the front pages of all the city and community newspapers. Dr. Bridgewater communicated that he was not only fighting for his human rights, but for the human rights of the employees, patients, and the communities that the hospital had been discriminating against for years. I started sending out my resume.

The protest lasted a few months and the hospital's administrators eventually sat down with him, their lawyers, and settled his lawsuit out of court. The hospital administrators didn't admit to his discrimination, retaliation and defamation of character charges, and didn't apologize, but they offered him back his medical privileges, which he declined.

Dr. Bridgewater was awarded a large settlement and created a medical scholarship fund for high school students who wanted to become future doctors. Dr. Bridgewater demonstrated to everyone that his lawsuit and the protest were not about the money, but that every employee and patient mattered.

Chapter 13

THE WHISTLE BLOWER

AFTER THE DRAMA, disagreements, and discrimination with Dr. Bridgewater had died down, it seemed like Urban Community Hospital was returning back to being serviceable again, but I was wrong. The majority of our patients departed to other competing hospitals and medical centers for their healthcare needs. The pressure on the hospital's marketers became excruciating. The hospital's employees, inpatient admissions, and senior programs started underperforming. The doctors became disappointed in the hospital's administrators and their inadequate leadership, unprofessionalism, decision making, and reduction in patients.

Whenever Waldo and I met, he seemed frustrated, and rumor has it, not happy. The gossip wire said that Waldo was overindulging on cocktails at home and enjoying expensive dinners and drinks after work with the new managers and computer guys, and paying the tabs with his hospital credit card. During all of the changes at the hospital, they hired Holly Davidson as the new Vice President of Nursing. She came from one of the community hospitals Waldo use to work at. She had over ten years of administrative nursing experience, exhibited enthusiasm, and was passionate about elevating nursing services.

The CEO became the invisible man who stayed in his office on most days and when we saw him, he was irritated. He appeared to have abandoned his hospital and employees and lost his swagger. After several months had gone by, the dysfunctional employees went back to being unhelpful, lackadaisical, and argumentative. They were empowered once again.

One early Wednesday morning, the F.B.I marched into the hospital with a subpoena and their guns drawn. The Medicare Fraud Strike Force, which is part of the Healthcare Fraud Prevention & Enforcement Action team (HEAT), a joint initiative between the U.S. Justice Department and the U.S. Department of Health and Human Services, filed a lawsuit on behalf of the state's Medicaid and Medicare programs for hospital fraud. They accused Urban Community Hospital and the CEO with fraudulent billing. They alleged that the hospital was overcharging Medicaid and Medicare for patient services they weren't providing for years.

The administrators, managers, employees, patients, and I, witnessed the F.B.I, the U.S. Justice Department, U.S. Department of Public Health, and Cook County State Police, confiscating and reviewing HR files, financial records, and patients' medical charts. They interviewed employees and ultimately visited and questioned patients at their homes. When the inspectors and investigators were present, the CEO had stopped walking the halls. I would see Waldo and Bernie in the cafeteria with the "mask of doom" on their faces. Helen, the VP of Geriatrics, supposedly grew ill and went on medical leave. The employees were confused, panicking and worried that they weren't going to get paid, and the hospital was going to have to padlock the doors and become another statistic.

The hospital gossip wire was whispering that the F.B.I. was investigating the hospital because of the way the CEO and his administration team treated Dr. Bridgewater. But, the truth of the matter was, that Urban Community had a whistleblower working with the F.B.I., and her name was Danielle Hartless. Danielle grew up in the community, was Alicia Keys fine, and had earned two master degrees. She contacted the family's lawyer and they reached out to the F.B.I. She discovered a number of inconsistencies in the patients coding from the accounting and billing departments, where she worked. The F.B.I had encouraged her to wear a wire.

Bernie had a little crush on Danielle and was always in her office, flirting and bragging. He informed her of how the hospital was accumulating millions of dollars from a foolproof system he personally designed for patient coding and billings. He unveiled to her how he altered the correct coding that the employees in the finance departments forwarded to him. He told how he resourcefully restructured the billing information the hospital charged to Medicare and Medicaid for patient services. Bernie truly believed that he was sharing his little creative secrets with a gorgeous co-worker, who he had his big green eyes on, but never realized he was running his big mouth to a mole with a big butt.

Once the employees found out who was really the initiator behind the investigation, they assumed Danielle blew the whistle on the administrators for ethical reasons, but once again we were wrong. Danielle's 66-year old father, a former United States Navy Seal, was admitted into Urban Community for an undiagnosed emergency.

The hospital treated the father and his family like they were the usual customers. They didn't have a clue that the patient was another employee's father. The employee's treatment towards the patient was despicable, uncaring, and unsatisfactory. The on-call physician came by earlier in the evening, examined him, and wrote the orders and prescription for the emergency pain medication, blood to be drawn, and a few critical tests that needed to be performed on him. His family left the hospital late at night assuming that his medical problems were going to be taken care of and by being in a hospital where his daughter worked, he was in good hands.

Danielle's father was scheduled for an emergency surgery the next day. During the night, the assigned nurse didn't make sure the medical technician's completed the necessary tests for the surgery. The father pushed his call button many times during the night because of the unbearable pain he was experiencing, but no one attended to him or gave him any pain medication. The call button was broken.

Danielle arrived at the hospital early the next morning and went to check on her father, and found him in the bed moaning from excruciating pain, and lying in his blood, urine, and feces. She went ballistic, cursing out the nurses around the nursing station. The nurses during the night were too busy sleeping, gossiping and laughing about the reality TV shows they watched on their smart phones. Her father was transferred to another hospital, immediately.

Danielle called her family members and they met at the other hospital. The next day, Danielle, the mother, Debbie, and her brother, Hakim, met with the CEO, Holly (the new VP of Nursing), and Waldo. The administrators were still trying to sweep the father's surgery blunders under the carpet. They informed Danielle and her family that they were reprimanding the nurses and employees who were responsible for the father's neglect, unacceptable service, and not carrying out their responsibilities. The administrators were embarrassed to have let one of their own employees down. Hakim vowed to sue the hospital and their mother seconded that emotion. Danielle felt that the hospital's abuse and neglectful treatment towards her father was unacceptable, unforgiveable, and unforgettable. Her father was not only a veteran, but a war hero. The father died a week later.

It took only one year for the F.B.I. and the Medicare Fraud Strike Force to scrutinize everything, and make their case against the CEO, Bernie, and Waldo. They were indicted for Medicaid and Medicare insurance fraud. The media and internet had a field day with the astonishing outcome. The Attorney General's office, the U.S Court system, and the Internal Revenue Service (IRS), charged the CEO and Bernie for not reporting their extra millions in revenue and income. The judgment against the hospital and the CEO was for $37 million dollars. The trial was settled out of court, because the CEO and Bernie pleaded guilty to all charges and Waldo's charges were dismissed for assisting the federal government with their case. The judge mandated the CEO to pay the court's judgment against the hospital, IRS and him without delay. It was reported by the media that the CEO was worth over $50 million dollars. The hospital was sold at an auction to a doctors group, but remained open for business. The employees, who weren't fired, remained employed to service the patients and the community.

Once the new owners took over Urban Community Hospital, the employees were awarded with a few new surprises. Dr. Bridgewater was one of the doctors in the physician group and became a co-owner. They quickly brought in an administrative transitional team and went to work. The CEO was put on probation for 15 years by the Federal Government and supposedly relocated to Miami, Florida, alone. He was banned for life by the Federal Government from owning a business and working in the healthcare industry.

Bernie, the VP of Finances, was prohibited to work in healthcare by the Federal Government as a part of his plea agreement and placed on the Federal Government's ban list, for life. The Government also banned Waldo, but he was not charged with any crimes, and not allowed to work for any healthcare company that had any business with the Federal Government. Holly, the new VP of Nursing, who was new and only along for the ride, Esther, the Director of Human Resources, and Helen, the VP of Geriatrics, and Dr. Murdock (the so-called slave master) were fired by the new owners.

Danielle, the celebrated whistleblower, was awarded 10% of the $37 million dollars that the government received back from the CEO and hospital. She instantaneously became a multi-millionaire and a Supershero to her family, the community, the government, and new fiancée. Her family never filed a lawsuit against the hospital.

A newspaper reporter asked Danielle, "Were you ever afraid that your plan to expose the hospital might not work?

Danielle proudly stated, "My father always told me that you can't have fear and faith at the same time. What the hospital and employees did to my father made God mad!"

The new CEO of Urban Community Hospital became Dr. America Rodriquez, the former VP of Geriatrics, and the creator of the hospitals seniors program. Everyone thought the former CEO had fired her, but because she disagreed with their unethical methods, she resigned. She went back to graduate school and completed her PhD in hospital administration.

Dr. Rodriquez promoted me to be the new Vice President of Marketing and Business Development. I'm glad I didn't resign during our challenging times because like they say, positive things happen to positive people. Every hospital employee was ecstatic about working with the new owners, their new board of directors, and new leadership, and providing excellent care and services to every patient. They also hired new primary care and specialty doctors, passionate managers, highly functioning employees, and an innovative marketing team, like no other.

The new owners changed the name of the hospital to New Hope Community Hospital. Today, it's a non-for-profit medical teaching institution that's training a new generation of doctors, nurses, and care givers to celebrate values, dedication, and teamwork. New Hope Community Hospital's vision is to be the gold standard in patient care and services, by treating patients with the most complex medical conditions and providing them with the finest clinical team, compassion, and treatment, ever.

New Hope Community remodeled the hospital with beautiful internal and external renovations, state-of-the-art technological medical equipment, and added a ground-breaking medical research team to enhance the clinical data, laboratories, programs and billing practices. The new mission will provide better care, employees, programs, resources, and services, to ensure that every patient receives five-star amenities and quality outcomes. The employees will be educated and coached by the top experts in the healthcare industry on the principles of customer service, cultural diversity, conflict resolutions, personal development, management, and business ethics.

New Hope's new ideas, changes, and actions will transform the employee's mind-set, culture, and camaraderie. Every employee will receive new raises, uniforms, and name tags, to increase their passion, production, and standards. The hospital created a medical clinic on wheels to provide free comprehensive medical services to community residents who don't have medical benefits. We built a food truck that will travel around the Chicagoland communities and give away warm nutritious meals and bags of groceries to the deprived. We purchased an old boarded up grocery store and renovated and reopened it as a fresh fruit and vegetable market. New Hope also purchased a lawn, landscaping and snow removing company to provide trainings and jobs for the community's residents and youth.

The community residents are renewing their attitudes and perceptions, which has motivated them to keep their homes, the parks, and community beautiful and immaculate. Law enforcement are supporting the community residents and forcing the urban terrorists, dope dealers and community offenders to change their destructive behavior or depart from the community. The inspired changes have made the community residents and children feel safer, caring and providing them with a community that is peaceful and looks just as attractive as the ones on TV and in the magazines.

New Hope Community Hospital is developing better relationships, partnerships, and sponsors to assist them in providing an annual health fair on our beautiful hospital grounds. The day of the first health fair, everybody came to celebrate the amazing success of New Hope Community, its community residents, the referral sources, ministers and their churches, community agency representatives, local and state politicians, the Governor, the Mayor, and the media.

The 44th President of the United States of America, Chicago's very own, President Barack Obama, was also invited. He was too busy implementing and perfecting the Affordable Care Act (Obama care), improving foreign policies, making sure all Americans were safe from gun violence, terrorists and global wars, revitalizing the immigration laws, restoring the economy with better paying jobs, re-educating a new generation of leaders, and making sure every American citizen lives the American dream. The White House sent a few astonishing representatives, the President's beautiful wife, first lady Michelle Obama, another Chicagoan, and the "Nations Doctor" Dr. Vivek Murthy, USA Surgeon General.

New Hope Community Hospital and the employees are accepting the new challenge to not only rebuild, restore and re-invent the hospital, themselves and healthcare initiatives, but to serve every customer with undying passion. The new mission is to use a patient first approach and be accountable for all of the patient's educational, emotional and spiritual needs. To deliver relationship centered empathy and keep the patients and employ-ees out of a dysfunctional workplace and teach them how to live a happy, healthy, and quality-driven lifestyle.

Today, we're thriving, celebrating and serving every patient, family, and the employees with a better focus, purpose and leg-acy, which will teach, inspire, and heal Chicago, America and the world... one dysfunctional state, city, community, business, hospital, leader, customer, and employee at a time.

Chapter 14

THE OUTCOME

WHAT A STORY, which I wrote with the intentions of exposing and educating you about the dysfunctional employees, leaders and managers working behind the scenes of an urban community hospital. My assignment was to empower you to take action, and rehabilitate our hospitals, employees, the workplace, and health-care industry.

While I was writing this book about a Dysfunctional Community Hospital, it taught me that it really wasn't about the hospital, the community, the employees, or the healthcare system, but that every employee needs to become more educated, functional and healthier in their minds, behavior, relationships, finances, and jobs, to live their God-given purpose. Whatever went on behind the doors at the Dysfunctional Community Hospital, or in your life, career, relationships and experiences is really metaphorical to what you need to achieve in your dysfunctional world.

One night I was watching a movie by one of my favorite directors and storytellers, Spike Lee, entitled: *Do the Right Thing!* The movie was a story about dysfunctional people who lived on a single block in the Brooklyn-Stuyvesant community with one white owned business, Sal's Famous Pizzeria, at the end of the block. The story had several dysfunctional characters and a racially polarized atmosphere which eventually erupted in racial violence on the hottest day of the year. The movie taught me and hopefully others about racism, stereotyping, anger, and violence and most importantly that everyone in the world has the power to do the right thing in adverse circumstances.

I believe that for you to re-invent, re-vitalize and re-empower yourself, you must continue to become the smartest, bravest and healthiest leader in this dysfunc-

> Spike Lee would say "Do the Right Thing," but I must say to always "Do a Smarter New Thing!"

tional, yet amazing world. Spike Lee would say "Do the Right Thing," but I must say to always "Do a Smarter New Thing!"

It may not be the next hot new thing to do or the new All-American cool, but when you "Do a Smarter New Thing" you lead by example, and implement smarter principles, programs, services and accountability, to help every employee become the smartest that they can possibly be. It's time to put our smarter new leadership, emotional intelligence, unquestionable character, and enduring tenacity into action, before it's too late.

How do we transform a Dysfunctional Hospital into a healthier, functioning and quality-driven hospital? The solutions are in your mind, hands and actions! We must create a smarter new hospital, smarter new leaders and managers and smarter new employees.

To be a Smarter New Hospital:

Provide smarter new leaders. Motivate and empower your leaders, managers and employees and the business and hospitals brand. Implement and advertise the mission, vision and value statements. Mandate positivity, professionalism, productivity and impeccable customer service, daily. Be proactive, transparent and ask employees profound questions and take time to listen and obtain results.

Invest in a health, wellness and counseling program. Develop and implement new initiatives that will promote employee healthy living, fitness and well-being programs and services. Present on-site health screenings, exercise groups, workout equipment and professional trainers. Motivate the employees to exercise and lose weight by bringing in instructors, experts and coaches to teach exercising fundamentals, Pilate classes and yoga and provide a room to achieve their new goals. Provide times throughout the day for ten-minute stretch breaks or overtime compensation when employees participate in after-hours activities.

Offer classes and workshops on nutrition, chronic illnesses, and stress and anger management. Provide smoking cessation classes. Give employees fitness wearables to build morale. Provide employees with the incentives to eat healthier by supplying the departments and break room refrigerators with healthy snacks, vegetables, fruit, water and non-sugar drinks. Incorporate healthy foods and a list of options in your cafeteria. Have a free salad day.

Create a confidential hot-line for employees (Employee Assistance Program) to call and talk to a professional expert about their personal problems and receive solutions, ideas and referrals. Incorporate a professional development coach and mental health counselor off-site. Provide role modeling classes to teach managers the professional behavior the hospital wants implemented to employees on how to treat each other and the customers. Provide a hospital Chapel, and prayer and meditation groups. Healthier employees are smarter and more responsible than dysfunctional and unhealthy employees.

Be a smarter new service provider. Put the employees (they're customers too), customers, business and hospital first. Invest in customized employee benefits and student loan management. Master the hospitals goals, plans and products and coach every employee. Be the expert in customer relations by providing customer service workshops. Teach the employees how to be relationship builders, customer friendly, accountable, compassionate, enthusiastic, and understanding of others. Utilize the hospitals evaluations, customer and employee service surveys, research data and the internet to know what the customer's and employees need, want and their communications in the workplace. Have a hug an employee day. Invest in your employees because without happy, healthy and productive employees the hospital, business and service would be substandard.

To be a Smarter New Manager:

Be insightful and supportive. It's the manager's responsibility to lead employees, departments and program's by being open-minded, flexible and mission focused. Look for new opportunities to be more supportive and productive. Encourage feedback from the employees in the trenches. Communicate frequently with the employees about their goals, plans, and projects. Let employees know when they make mistakes and help them make corrections. Make sure the employees are motivated and successful by measuring their goals, objectives and results. Offer praise and criticize constructively, not destructively. Use your talents, experience and expertise to assist and support every employee who works in your department and the hospital. Manage and treat employees the way you would like to be treated.

Re-educate and invest in yourself. Master the business rules, policies, regulations and operations and educate your co-workers. Learn the EEOC (Equal Employee Office Commission) human, equal and civil right laws to gain more knowledge and be a better educator and role-model. Coordinate and facilitate cultural diversity and inclusion, discrimination, conflict resolutions, sexual harassment, ethnics, and team building trainings. Be committed and learn how to support and counsel an employee in problematical times. Learn how to be a mentor or professional development trainer to the employees. Be a better interviewer when hiring employees by asking insightful and behavioral questions designed to reveal candidate's personal values. Take a stress and anger management class to manage your emotions. Have meetings with a purpose and listen to the employee's ideas for new solutions.

Be mission-driven. The mission should be to solve customers' problems, provide impeccable customer service and give back to the community. Memorize the business's mission statement and perform it daily. Talk about the mission and keep it in front of you to remind yourself and every employee that the customer is always #1! Set smarter new goals and develop a new plan of action. Be a team leader and encourage teamwork to increase productivity, profitability and impeccable outcomes. Promote teamwork to be on the same page and solve difficult problems. Cross train each employee to share their skills and expertise with their team members, so everyone will know how to do each other's jobs. Embrace diversity and inclusion. Stop judging leadership, employees, the customers and yourself. Work with passion and let it keep you motivated, enthusiastic and accommodating to others.

To be a Smarter New Employee:

Reinvent yourself. Be open-minded and learn something new every day. Ask questions because the person who asks questions will know the answers. Read books and magazines on self-improvement, psychotherapy and finances. Take professional development classes. Invest in a life coach because the more training and experiences you have, the more options you'll have. Participate in an Employee Assistance Program or talk to a mental health counselor, confidentially. Join a drug and alcohol program or support group. Communicate your issues with family members, friends, a mentor or spiritual advisor. Pray, mediate and breathe, it's your connection to the creator. Attend church or a faith base organization. Be a volunteer.

Learn in-demand skills for your job and the new career trends for the future. Learn guest relations, diverse languages, and leadership. Upgrade your technological aptitude and skills by studying hi-tech books, taking new software classes, and learning online and with the newest business and social apps, video conferencing and webinars.

Be accountable. It's your responsibility to be the smartest, nicest and healthiest employee that you can be. Renew your attitude to transform your thinking, behavior, perception, success and help you keep your head in the game. Learn how to accept leadership, constructive criticism and coaching. Be professional, likeable and smile. Be teachable, coachable, confident and enthusiastic by learning from other extraordinary leaders in the work place. Embrace team work and be a team player. Keep your promises and don't be a procrastinator. Demonstrate to the business, managers and customers that you are unfailing, dedicated and responsible. Manage your time by being punctual. Speak, write and communicate with a new purpose. Say something and do something when things are not ethical. Be trustworthy and make the decision to trust your leaders, co-workers, the service process, and yourself. Embrace your brand new assignments with confidence and passion. Be proactive, adaptable, and dependable and prepared. Be the problem solver and fix the problem, but don't be the problem.

Participate in a health, fitness and wellness program. How can you help your company, co-workers and the customers if you're not taking care of you? The business and hospital you work for is dependent on you taking care of your life, health, responsibilities, and work assignments. Visualize yourself looking fit, feeling healthy, stress free and enjoying your healthy new future. Tune up your body, see a physician, get a physical and take all the necessary tests for hypertension, high cholesterol, cancers, diabetes, and for women a mammogram exam.

Transform your destructive habits (abusing fast foods and sugary sodas, energy drinks, alcohol, prescription drugs, heroin, cocaine, crack, marijuana, cigarettes, and cigars), into constructive habits (exercising, jogging, walking, swimming, dancing, vacationing, eating healthier, drinking purified water, sleeping, and working on your dreams and hobbies).

Tell a brand new story and inspire someone. Stop making excuses and get into action. Never give up, give in or give out. Celebrate and value your mind, body and spirit and they will take better care of you.

Remember once we invest in the leaders, employees and customers, it will energetically teach everyone how to be smarter, healthier, productive and service-driven. I would like to personally salute, honor, congratulate and celebrate you for being a highly functional employer, leader, manager and employee, instead of a dysfunctional one.

This is your smarter new life, season and future, produce like it.

The End!

Thank you and God bless you and your legacy.

EXIT!

ABOUT THE AUTHOR

MICHAEL ABRAHAM APPLEGATE is an inter-nationally re-nowned motivational speaker, empowerment program specialist and an author. Michael's four books *"Making Dreams Happen, Raising a Brand New Bar, Please Stop the Violence and The Prescriptions for Impeccable Customer Service!"* are best sellers and teaches individuals how to celebrate their life, dreams, health, purpose, service and legacy.

Michael has over 25 years of experience and expertise in self-improvement, healthcare, marketing, business development and programs and services for executives, employees, service providers, parents and today's youth.

Michael is known as *"The Energizer"* and specializes in impeccable customer service, employee development, leadership, job training, sales and marketing, team work, financial literacy, relationship building, cultural diversity, violence prevention, conflict resolutions, and achieving extraordinary results.

Michael's mission is to educate, motivate, and provide interactive programs and services that will teach the prescriptions, principles, strategies, and tools to empower individual's how to live happy, healthy, wealthy and destiny-driven lives.

The greatest service I can offer is to…
Elevate the Next Generation of Service Providers!

ACKNOWLEDGMENTS

I WOULD LIKE TO THANK my phenomenal and loving family Debra, Mike Jr., Brittany, mother Dorothy Mae, father Abraham Washington and sisters and brothers. Thanks to my angels who are disguised as my mentors, role models, supporters and friends (too many to name, but they know who they are).

Thanks to the CEO's, employees, co-workers, colleagues, volunteers and teachers for educating, motivating and serving in our hospitals, businesses, communities, churches, schools and this extraordinary world.

Thanks to Chris DeGuire, adjunct faculty in the Department of Creative Writing at Columbia College Chicago (cdeguire. wordpress.com). Thanks to Jim and Barbara Weems of "The Book Producers" for making my books beautiful.

Thanks to our almighty God (my CEO, Father and Friend) for providing me with new ideas, gifts, purpose, and work ethic to be a relentless service provider in a customer-driven world.

Hug yourself for your Impeccable Service!

Invest in Someone and Donate a Book!

Have you made any rewarding investments lately? Why not invest in someone. An investment is an opportunity to deposit constructive, healthy and profitable knowledge into someone's life, world and experiences. What better way to educate, motivate and elevate someone's dreams, career and future, than by giving them a book of stories, principles, ideas, tools and action steps to mega-success. You can donate any book to someone and please do, but why not my smarter new books.

Make a life-changing contribution by purchasing and donating my new books, today:

Dysfunctional Community Hospital:
An Inside Story of Dysfunctional Employees at Work!

Please Stop the Violence:
How to Save a Life, a Generation and America!

The Prescriptions For Impeccable Customer Service:
Elevate your Job, Mission and Service in a Customer-Driven World!

Each smarter new book is only $9.99 each (shipping and handling is free). Contact Michael at www.MichaelAApplegate.com. Make an investment and change a generation.

Looking for a Motivational Speaker, Professional Development Trainer or Business Consultant? Contact Michael *"The Energizer"* Applegate at www.MichaelAApplegate.com

Thank you!

YOUR JOURNAL!

_____

_____

_____

_____

_____

_____

_____

_____

_____

_____

_____

_____

_____

_____

_____

_____

_____

_____

_____

_____

_____

_____

_____

_____

YOUR JOURNAL!

www.ingramcontent.com/pod-product-compliance
Lightning Source LLC
Chambersburg PA
CBHW071333130626
46556CB00004B/1885